Dalliance with the Duchess

Disgraceful Duchesses, Book 3

Sara Bennett

Dragonblade Publishing, Inc. is an imprint of Kathryn Le Veque Novels, Inc.
P.O. Box 23
Moreno Valley, CA 92556
ceo@dragonbladepublishing.com

Produced in the United States of America

First Edition November 2024
Trade Paperback Edition

ARE YOU SIGNED UP FOR DRAGONBLADE'S BLOG?

You'll get the latest news and information on exclusive giveaways, exclusive excerpts, coming releases, sales, free books, cover reveals and more.

Check out our complete list of authors, too!

No spam, no junk. That's a promise!

Sign Up Here

www.dragonbladepublishing.com

Dearest Reader;

Thank you for your support of a small press. At Dragonblade Publishing, we strive to bring you the highest quality Historical Romance from some of the best authors in the business. Without your support, there is no 'us', so we sincerely hope you adore these stories and find some new favorite authors along the way.

Happy Reading!

CEO, Dragonblade Publishing

Additional Dragonblade books by Author Sara Bennett

Disgraceful Duchesses Series
Seducing the Duchess (Book 1)
Tempting the Duchess (Book 2)
Dalliance with the Duchess (Book 3)

Chapter One

SOPHIA SHUT THE door on the party with a sense of relief and turned to face the room. It was smallish, with comfortable chairs and shelves stuffed with books, and it had an air of calm. Exactly what she craved. The chatter and laughter had seemed overwhelming for one who had spent most of the past year in mourning. Had she once enjoyed these Society dos? When she had first joined the *ton*, newly married to Oldney, hungry for the excitement of grand occasions, she had wanted to savor every single moment. The intrigue and the gossip, those were the things she had lived for. It had felt like all her dreams had come true—if you took out the part where she was married to a man as despicable as the Duke of Oldney.

Oldney had been a good deal older than her—almost forty—and had never planned to marry. But he told her he had been dazzled by her beauty. She had never loved him, though. Any girlish imaginings in that respect had been quashed very quickly, but he had kept her on a tight rein. No lovers for her at any point during their decade of marriage. Even his best friends received a sharp rebuke if they strayed into familiarity.

But now Oldney was dead and, as his widow, suddenly Sophia was free to do very much as she pleased.

The trouble was she had no interest in being the woman she

had been before. Oldney's corrupt and dangerous set no longer interested her. It was as if, up until now, the constant round of engagements had kept her from thinking at all. But once they had stopped and she was forced into seclusion, the awful truth began to reveal itself to her.

She hated her life. She felt empty. And she did not know what to do about it.

The click of the door opening brought her out of her dismal thoughts. Irritably she turned to face the intruder. A man stood in the doorway, silhouetted against the colorful crush in the other room. Someone's high-pitched laughter sent a painful jangle through her head, making her wince.

"This room is occupied," she said, perhaps not as politely as she should have.

Instead of leaving her in peace, the man closed the door behind him.

"Sir, I am not in the mood for company."

He ignored her, moving forward until the light of the table lamp fell over him. That was when she recognized him. Her heart gave a jump, and a tingle ran all the way down to her toes.

Nicholas Blake.

A man she had hated from the moment she'd met him. Last year he had helped her sister, Ellis, escape a dangerous situation, and although she was grateful to him for that, she still had not come to like him.

And then, three months ago, she had met him again, and the less said about *that* meeting the better. Especially as her identity had been hidden behind a mask and he still did not know it was Sophia he had encountered that night.

Now he was staring back at her consideringly, as if he was making his mind up about something. Sophia kept her face blank—she had learned over the years that it did not serve her well to give her emotions free reign.

But inside it was a different matter. Inside she was a tangled mess of feelings she could not begin to name. She just knew that the sight of him, tall and dark haired, his head slightly bent as he judged her with those serious brown eyes under his heavy brows, caused a tremor inside her chest. Yes, he was a striking man, there was no denying it, and she was not immune to his looks despite telling herself she was.

She did not want to feel like this. But ever since that night . . .

No, Sophia would not let herself think of that now!

"Your Grace." Belatedly he bowed. "I apologize for disturbing your moment of reflection, but I wanted to speak to you in private."

Sophia stood up and gave him a haughty stare. "What can you possibly have to say to me, in private or otherwise, Mr. Blake?"

He came closer still, and she couldn't help but notice his skintight beige pantaloons and his blue evening jacket. He had never dressed gaudily, to bring notice to himself, but Sophia had always thought him one of the most elegantly dressed men in any room in which he was present.

His hands on her naked thighs, his mouth on hers, the first thrust of his cock into her warm, welcoming body . . .

The raw image shocked her and she shoved it away. This was neither the time nor place for such memories. Surely she was not still mooning over a man she had coupled with three months ago? At the time she had been lonely, craving company, and he had seemed just as eager. It had been nothing, had meant nothing, and she certainly had no desire to ever do it again.

She ignored the throb inside her body while she waited impatiently for him to speak.

He was so close now that she could see the smooth, clean-shaven skin of his face, and his long dark eyelashes. She could smell him too, the warm scent of his spicy pomade, and the male scent of *him*. Of Nicholas Blake, whom, she reminded herself again, she hated.

Although what she was feeling at this moment did not seem like hate, or if it were then it was mixed in with a large dose of lust.

"Did you get my letter after Oldney died? I wrote to you expressing my condolences."

"I tore it up and burned it. My late husband despised you, Mr. Blake. You have spent years trying to bring him down, and no doubt, if he had not dropped dead of an apoplexy, you would still be at it."

He nodded slowly. "You are probably right. Oldney and I were worlds apart. But I did not come here to speak to you of the late duke. Will you grant me a moment of your time, Your Grace?"

She just wanted him to go away. The memory of the masked ball popped back into her head, and there it was again—the wet heat of his mouth, the unbearable ache of wanting, and the almost rough pleasure as he took her in the shadows of the arbor.

Her nipples pebbled painfully hard, and she hoped the thin silk of her bodice hid them from his watchful eyes.

"If you insist. Tell me what you want quickly, and then leave." She sounded suitably chilly, and she knew her beautiful face would be as unapproachable as ever.

His mouth turned down at the corners and his shoulders lifted in a shrug. "I need your help," he said.

It was unexpected, and she stared. "My *help*?"

"I can see you are surprised," he mocked, but she thought it was himself he was mocking. "How could you not be? I have surprised myself. But it is true. There is no one who knows more about the inner secrets of Oldney's old set than Your Grace."

"It has been a year since I was part of that set. I have been a widow in mourning." Although Sophia was sure some of those gentlemen would have been more than happy to welcome her so that they could enjoy scandalizing Society even more than they already did. "Why do you need to know about Oldney's set?"

"I am interested in one member in particular. He started fraternizing with them two months ago. Sir Gordon Robinson. Do you know him?"

She shook her head, bemused. She might have reminded him

once more that she had been out of circulation for a year, but he was already speaking again.

"Sir Gordon is known to me. He was a neighbor, and although he is younger than I, we were always good friends. Or I thought so, at least. I was looking forward to resuming that friendship when he arrived in town, but these past months . . . he has decided there is more amusement to be found in the sorts of pursuits Oldney's old set indulges in. I am worried about him."

"So it is a personal matter?" No wonder Blake was unsettled. Bad enough that he was unable to remove his friend from such a vicious group of gentlemen, but that he had to ask *her* for help had to be galling. It must sting a man as self-sufficient and arrogant as Nicholas Blake.

"The last time I spoke to him we argued. Badly. Now he will not listen to me. If you could approach him and let me know how he is, if you can let me know if you think he needs rescuing . . ."

"So that you can rescue him?" she said dryly. "I see."

He was watching her carefully, as if reading the thoughts circling around in her head, although Sophia knew that was not possible. She had become too adept at hiding them. But she considered his surprising request. She could refuse him in such an insulting way that he would never ask her again, and she was within her rights to do that. Basically, he was asking her to spy upon her friends, although in truth, "friends" was rather overstating it. Oldney had been an awful man. He had made her life very unhappy, and she wasn't in the least bit upset that he was dead. As for the others . . . She pictured their faces—vicious, depraved men who cared for nothing but their own pleasure and amusement. They had welcomed her into their group where she had watched them destroy lives, and she had not lifted a finger. How could she, when it would have lost her everything? Her place in Society would have been in jeopardy. Oldney would have cast her aside and sent her to live in the country. The invitations to everything that had seemed important to her would have dried up.

She had been selfish.

One particular memory preyed upon her mind—a young and foolish girl who had believed one of Oldney's friends, the Marquess of Chatham, was in love with her and was going to ask for her hand. She had been ruined at a ball when several guests walked into a room where she was spread out beneath the marquess. He hadn't married her and had even laughed when asked if he had ever intended to do so. Society did not like what he had done, but he was not censured because he was a titled gentleman. Sophia did not know what had happened to the girl, and usually she tried not to think about it.

She was thinking about it now.

And what of this Sir Gordon Robinson, caught up in their web? She had been that person once, and she had only been safe because she was Oldney's possession. What would have happened to her if she had not been married to him? She had done nothing to help the girl at the time—Indeed, what could she have done?—and she did feel guilty about it. The distance of a year had shown her with painful clarity how wrong the behavior of that set had been, and how her silence had made her an accessory in the affair. Was this an opportunity to make reparation for her inaction in that and all the other things she had seen and pretended not to?

Blake was still watching her, no doubt expecting the worst. It had taken courage to ask her at all, and reluctantly she admired him for that. "Why should I help you?" she asked curiously.

He almost smiled. "You helped your sister when she was in trouble. You cared about her. I think beneath the ice queen demeanor you have feelings, Your Grace. Am I wrong?"

Had he really seen a part of her she had thought so well hidden? Or was he manipulating her to get his way? "I will consider your request," she said coolly. "It requires some thought."

His face brightened, as if he were relieved she had not refused him out of hand. He bowed and said, "Thank you. I am most grateful, Your Grace. Should I call on you tomorrow? Perhaps at

10 o'clock, to discuss the matter further?"

Oh, he was keen. She waved a dismissive hand. "I am engaged all day tomorrow."

He murmured his disappointment. She met his dark gaze and a tremor ran through her, and it made her reckless. "Call on me tomorrow evening and we can discuss the matter over supper."

He looked as surprised at hearing the words as she was dismayed at saying them. What was she thinking? He would refuse her, wouldn't he? But no, of course he wouldn't. He needed her it seemed, and for now she had him at her beck and call. It was an unexpectedly heady feeling and was clearly skewing her judgement.

"As Your Grace wishes," he said politely, but his eyes were curious, searching her face as if he was trying to understand her better.

"Then it is a date," she replied. "Now, if you are finished, I would prefer my own company, Mr. Blake."

His mouth twitched. "Apologies, Your Grace." He bowed again before walking away.

The door closed.

Sophia sank down on a chair and made a little sound of distress. Madness. It must be. She had always claimed to hate Nicholas Blake, so why would she put herself in his company over an intimate supper?

And why couldn't she forget that night, that wonderful dreadful night, three months ago?

Chapter Two

Three months ago, Vauxhall Pleasure Gardens

As Sophia passed the pavilion, she smoothed the lace on her sleeves and glanced down to make sure her bodice was still high enough to confine her breasts. Her emerald-green gown was daring, but like a lot of other visitors to the gardens, she was wearing a full face mask, and she doubted anyone would know her.

These night affairs at Vauxhall Gardens were known to be scandalous. Certainly, if one was worried about one's reputation, it was a good place to stay away from, but Sophia was experienced enough in the ways of the *ton* to tread carefully. She knew it was rather shocking for a widow to be out like this, but over the past months she had felt a growing need to do something other than mourn a husband who was as much a stranger to her dead as he had been alive. She needed to mingle with other people, to feel *alive* again, or she would begin to climb the walls of her Berkeley Square town house.

She had tried to love Oldney, although she had never managed it. He had certainly never loved her. He had controlled her, or at least he had attempted to do so, and Sophia had soon learned to keep her own council when it came to her thoughts and emotions, giving him less to work with. She may have been the lesser partner in their marriage, but by keeping a part of herself free of his interference, she had tried to retain something of the girl she had once been. She was not entirely successful. He was always there, observing, informing her in his cool, precise manner that she was not to do this or that. Oldney may be dead, but it was taking her longer than she had hoped to shake off the past. Even now she found herself looking over her shoulder, to see if he was still watching.

And while it was true she did not want her old life back, hiding away and pretending to mourn felt as if she was letting Oldney win even in his absence. She was sick and tired of it. She needed to get out, to walk among others, to feel her spirits lift. Surely, as long as she was not recognized, no one could accuse her of improper behavior? Sophia wanted to step outside the cage Oldney had built for her, to reclaim that optimistic girl she had been. Once she had broken free, she was sure she could finally put him behind her.

A laughing group brushed against her but barely seemed to notice her. The pleasure gardens were filling up, and music drifted over the groups of excited people attending. Rich and poor mingled, and Sophia lost herself in the crush. She felt a little like a ghost, invisible to her fellow revelers.

Lamps of a countless number of colors shone from trees and along colonnades. Sophia wandered, soaking in her freedom. Beside the pavilion a woman shrieked with laughter and some inebriated gentlemen guffawed. Sophia slipped by them, looking about for somewhere to sit and watch the dancers. She spotted a rotunda with a good view and moved toward it.

And that was when she saw him.

He was masked, but the mask only covered half his face, from eyes to nose, leaving the lower half free. And Sophia knew those lips. How many times had she watched them opening and closing, polite words spilling out of them while the intent behind them was anything but polite? She had watched them curve in a mocking smile or tighten in anger. Her hatred of Nicholas Blake was well known, but there had been times when her anger at him had risen from a simmer to a boiling point and made her feel as if she was about to explode. As if . . . as if he only had to touch her and she would combust. What was that? She'd tried to dismiss it, because deep inside she suspected that feeling was dangerous, that she must never let him get too close to her. And there were occasions when he looked at her, his dark eyes aglitter, when she had wondered if he felt the same.

Blake had been a long-standing enemy of Sophia's husband, and Oldney had loathed him for being a "commoner" who had the audacity to look down his nose at his "betters."

"He only gets away with it because he is useful to his friends in the government, so they tolerate him."

But Blake had done what Sophia was too afraid to do, and that was to say something to Oldney's set about that girl Chatham had ruined. His words to them had been scathing and on point, and the aristocrats had not taken his rebuke well. Even before that they had been enemies, but afterward that enmity had turned into a deep and personal loathing.

Sophia had followed her husband's lead, her animosity for Blake building over time. It was a useful façade when she suspected her feelings weren't so cut and dried. He was a mystery to her, and she had found herself wanting to know more. But it was a dangerous preoccupation. Whenever she was in his company, she was aware of an unwelcome spark. It was best ignored, and when she couldn't ignore it, she redoubled her efforts to hate him.

And now here he was, Nicholas Blake at the Vauxhall Pleasure Gardens, looking about him as if he was expecting to see someone. No doubt he was on one of his missions for whoever it was who owned him. She had never been sure who that was, although Oldney had believed Blake would toil for whichever government paid him the most to do their dirty work.

Sophia had always wholeheartedly agreed, aloud anyway, but

she wasn't quite able to convince herself Blake was that immoral. Would he have castigated Chatham and the others for their treatment of the girl at the ball if he was so completely without moral feeling? It seemed to her that rather than being the corrupt blackguard Oldney had believed him to be, Blake was one of those puritanical types who saw everything in black and white. He was a do-gooder with tyrannical tendencies.

Now, her thoughts ground to a halt as his gaze went over her, paused, and then moved on. Sophia wasn't sure whether to be relieved or disappointed that she hadn't warranted more attention than that. *Relieved* she told herself, with a shrug of her shoulders. The musicians had started up again and she decided she would not sit and watch after all. Where was the fun in that? Instead she would find someone to dance with and enjoy herself until it was time to return home to her big, empty house.

It didn't take long for Sophia to find a partner, although he seemed to want to talk. At first it *was* fun, and she was skillful enough to evade his questions as to her identity, but then it began to grow wearisome. He would not accept her need to remain a mystery. She was relieved when the dance finished, and she made her excuses and turned away, only to find Nicholas Blake standing directly behind her.

Her heart gave an unwelcome thump and she had the urge to run away, which she quelled. Sophia never ran away from anything.

He looked down at her, his dark eyes glittering through his mask, and she read interest in them, and a challenge. "Mysterious lady," he said, with a teasing grin, "will you dance with me?"

There was a moment when she might have refused, or simply brushed by him, but she found she did not want to. He couldn't know who she was, and suddenly it seemed like an excellent joke to pretend she was a stranger and to dance with him. She bit back a smile as she imagined the look of chagrin on his face if he ever discovered her true identity. But he wouldn't, because how could he?

Without a word, Sophia went into his arms.

He was taller than she, and his cravat was at eye level—plainly tied crisp white linen. Elegant. She could smell his soap or his pomade, something like cinnamon or nutmeg. Delicious. His arm was around her waist, strong enough to make her feel as if she was floating as they danced, while his other hand clasped hers in a firm grip.

It was good. Better than she could have imagined. And if her inner voice was whispering about danger, then she ignored it. One dance finished and another one started. She wanted to keep dancing with him all night, twirling through the crowd, their bodies brushing against each other.

"Do I know you?"

His question startled her out of her thoughts. She shook her head, and then shrugged for good measure. He laughed softly, a huff of breath, and his dark eyes shone as they dipped to the swell of her breasts rising over the bodice of her gown.

"That is the point of these things, I suppose, isn't it?" he said. "To keep one's identity a secret."

She smiled again, thinking it safer not to speak, as he'd heard her voice many times. He clearly did not recognize her, but it was best not to take any chances.

His mouth twitched into a smile. "I didn't expect to enjoy myself here tonight, Mysterious Lady. But all business and no pleasure can be rather dull. Don't you agree?"

Sophia did agree. His arm about her waist tightened, pulling her in against him. Her skirts were diaphanous enough to leave no doubt as to his arousal. If it had been anyone else she would have extracted herself and given him a cold stare, but this was Nicholas Blake. Her body tingled with sensation, and she felt quite lightheaded. She had come here in a bid to feel alive again and it was an unexpected treat that she should meet the very man who always brought her heated emotions to the fore.

Her hand glided along the shoulder of his jacket, feeling the bone and muscle beneath, and curled about his nape. She slid her fingers up into his hair, the short strands soft—she wanted to keep touching them. Sophia had always wondered what his hair would feel like. She had always wondered what it would be like to kiss him, too, but to do that she must remove her mask and she was not that reckless.

He reached down to grasp her hips, leaned in even closer, and she was shockingly aware of the hard shape of him, pressing against her most sensitive of places. She gasped, arching against him. It had been so long since a man had held her and touched her, and she had never been held and touched by a man she desired. Because it was true, she *did* desire him. As much as she had tried to fight it in the past, Sophia was relieved now to admit it.

There was a whisper of breath against her ear, sending shivers over her skin.

"Do you want to go somewhere more private?"

She supposed she should be repelled by his forwardness, but he was only giving voice to her own wishes. A shiver of pleasure and excitement had her looking up at him coyly through the holes in her mask. He was still smiling, and she could see he desired her, too. For Sophia, knowing who he was while he didn't recognize her made their encounter all the more titillating.

Who did he imagine her to be? Some lady of the night, or a bored wife or mistress? Someone who was audacious enough to seek out a rendezvous with a stranger? Sophia could play that part; indeed, she found she was looking forward to it.

She opened her mouth to answer, and then nodded instead. The muscles in his arm tensed and then he released her, and with a flourish held out his hand. When she placed hers in it, his fingers gripped tight. And then he was leading her away from the dancers and down a path that took them deep into the gardens.

Vauxhall was notorious for its grottos and secluded nooks, and the trysts that were conducted there. No one would care, no one would look at them, and besides, no one knew who she was. Probably no one knew who Nicholas Blake was either. She herself had only recognized him because it seemed over the past few years he had become a permanent thorn in her husband's side. And consequently hers.

There were small lamps strung through the trees, flickering like starlight, just bright enough to illuminate their way. Murmurs came from her left, and a gasping cry from her right. She did not look but it made her hesitate. Should she turn back? This seemed a risky venture even for the Dowager Duchess of Oldney. But then she asked herself: Who was there to care?

She wanted to *feel* again, and right now she felt more alive than she had for years.

Ahead of her, Nicholas had paused, and then with a glance at her, led them toward what looked to be a trimmed arch of greenery. There was a seat within it, hidden from prying eyes, and he drew her down beside him. As he went to lift her mask, she caught his hand hard in hers and shook her head.

"No kissing then?" he said, more of a statement than a question. "At least . . . not on the face."

It occurred to Sophia that he was quite determined to have his way with her. Was this something he did regularly, prowl the pleasure gardens seeking women? It seemed unlikely, and certainly she had never thought so—the opposite in fact. Would he wish his reputation to be tarnished by such behavior? She knew he was not married, but perhaps he kept a mistress. And yet, once again, she did not think he would do that—betray a woman he held dear—but perhaps she was being foolishly naïve.

"Where did you go?"

Startled, she turned to him and realized he was watching her and had probably said something she hadn't heard. "I'm right here," she whispered.

"I should have brought a bottle of champagne," he said. Then, with a hint of concern, "Would you prefer to return?" He stood up, ready to escort her back to the noise and dancers.

But Sophia did not want to go back. Boldly she reached to press her hand to the fall of his pantaloons, against the swell of his cock.

He went still and she saw him bite his lip.

She ran her fingers over him, and then began to unbutton him. Slowly, watching the play of his mouth and the way his eyes closed behind the half mask, she slid her hand inside his pantaloons and took a firm hold of him.

He groaned and pushed against her. He was hard and getting harder. Clearly this sort of thing was to his taste.

Sophia wasn't about to suck him, but she was aching for him to touch and kiss her, to let her ride him mindlessly to the oblivion she craved.

And why not? He seemed keen to play along. Perhaps they were just two lonely people, and there was nothing wrong in needing human contact. Nothing dangerous at all.

Sophia stood up, too, and pushed him back onto the seat. He sat down with a grunt, staring up at her in surprise. She began to draw up her skirts, bunching them around her thighs. Her stockings were tied above her knees, so there was nothing to impede her as she knelt on the bench, one knee either side of him, and reached down to take hold of his cock.

His hands fumbled at her hips, clasping her and then lifting her, and she felt the tip brush against her entrance. She was slick with desire, but he was big and she held her breath as she slid down onto him. Slowly. Until he was inside her completely.

There were beads of sweat on his top lip, and his fingers clenched on her, as if he found it difficult to be still. She wriggled to settle herself, and he dropped his head to hers with a groan. "You're killing me," he said.

"If only that were true," she whispered.

She felt him still, staring at her, and knew she shouldn't have said it. Too late now. To distract him she moved up on his shaft, and then down again, repeating the movement, and feeling the glide against her most sensitive parts. She wanted to continue that slow slide, building toward what she already knew would be an astonishing culmination. But then he began to thrust into her, pinning her to him so that he could gain maximum benefit. That was good, too, but better when she leaned forward so that the slide of his member could rub firmly against her swollen bud, giving her the most pleasure.

Even so, she couldn't get it quite right, and made a frustrated sound, just as his hand pushed under her skirts and found her. He cupped her, and then circled her with his thumb, and desire sparked bright. She whimpered.

"You like that," he growled. "Don't want to kill me now, eh?"

Sophia ignored his provocative words, moving more quickly now, just as he was. Her climax was building, building, and oh so close, and then everything went into freefall. She trembled and shook in his arms, clinging to him and barely aware of him following her with a deep, satisfied groan.

For a time they panted, not moving. As if at a distance, she heard the sounds of other couples enjoying themselves. An owl called, flying low overhead and as if far away, the music continued to play.

She felt marvelous. Her body was relaxed, her mind was clear. It was the best she had felt since Oldney had died and left her in limbo.

Nicholas Blake's breathing was slowing, warm against her shoulder, and she realized they had not even bothered to undress. Probably just as well—it made the encounter even less personal. And yet she felt a tingle of disappointment, too. She would have liked to see him naked, felt his skin against hers, his mouth devouring hers . . .

"What is your perfume?" he asked, his voice gravelly, as he lifted his head.

"Honeysuckle," she said without thinking.

When he didn't reply, she rose to her feet and straightened her skirts. He began to tuck himself away before he also stood. They faced each other and there was an awkward silence.

"Can we meet again?" he asked suddenly. "I find myself craving another meeting."

That was a surprise. A surprise too that she wanted to agree.

"Better not," Sophia finally whispered, more to herself than him.

He sighed and then bowed. "As you wish," he said.

A moment later she was hurrying back along the path, toward the pavilion. She would leave, there was no point in staying now. She felt a thrill of amazement at her own daring.

She had been intimate with Nicholas Blake! It felt like an amazing victory, a fine jest. A pity he would never know who she was.

And at the same time a warning was sounding in her head. She had opened a door that should probably have remained closed. Why then could she not feel regret?

Chapter Three

The Present

THE DAY HAD been a long one. Sophia had a morning meeting with Oldney's man of business and estate manager, Thatcher. He was a dislikable fellow and every time she had to put up with his company she promised herself she would find someone new. At first she had felt out of her depth when it came to financial matters, and Thatcher's smirk as she frowned down at the ledgers didn't help, but she soon realized she could not possibly do a worse job than her late husband had.

Things had been dire when she picked up the baton, but she had made headway, economizing to slowly bring Oldney's estates back from the brink of disaster, although there was a long way to go yet.

Sophia knew how she was spoken about—the beautiful but poor Mallory girl who was lifted to dizzying heights by marrying a duke. Others would not expect someone who came from poverty—one they believed had nothing to recommend them but their looks—to be capable of managing Oldney's finances. But she had enjoyed proving them wrong just as much as she had enjoyed learning new skills and being able to navigate this new stage of her life.

As for those who envied Sophia's luck in landing a duke in the first place . . . By the time she had been married a fortnight, Sophia had known that neither tears nor pleas would work with her duke—he enjoyed seeing her weep and beg—and the only way she could survive as his wife was to be an ice queen who cared for nothing and nobody. That was how she fit in with Oldney's set of friends, too—by becoming just as outwardly vicious and selfish as they were.

And now Nicholas Blake was asking her to return to that life, and a sense of guilt—a conscience she had always tried to bury— was urging her to agree. At least in principle, as he was yet to discuss with her the full story of his friend. But could she do it, even if she wanted to?

For a start, she would have to make herself presentable now she was out of mourning. Appearing in public again in an out-of-date dress would make her a laughingstock. She sent a note to her modiste to make an appointment, telling herself that it did not mean she would agree to whatever Blake wanted her to do, but at least if she did then she would be ready.

She admitted to herself that the thought of those gentlemen who had been Oldney's closest companions made her feel queasy. The Marquess of Chatham, Lord Butcher, and Sir Tomas Arnold. Only three of them now, but no doubt just as unpleasant as they had always been. Sophia feared she had lost her hard edge, her ability to play her part, and it might be a struggle to get it back again. She wasn't sure who she was now, but she knew she did not want to be that woman anymore. Sometimes she felt like a stranger to herself.

As the day went on, as an additional irritant, her housekeeper left her to return home after an urgent message from her ailing mother. Sophia had even offered her a higher salary to stay but without success. It seemed familial loyalty overrode greed. Webster, her butler, gave her a mournful look when she informed him they would all just have to make do.

"You are quite capable of ordering the servants until we find someone else, Webster."

"Very well, Your Grace," the butler said, while the twist of his mouth said something else altogether.

By supper time, Sophia was on tenterhooks about Nicholas Blake's visit. She *was* curious as to exactly what he wanted from her. Who was this friend of his who needed rescuing? And was she really the only person who could help him? Her conscience was tapping on her shoulder again, but she did her best to ignore it, and told herself she would make her decision when he had explained everything.

As for their encounter at Vauxhall . . . it was long forgotten. Well, that was what she told herself, but the truth was she remembered it far too well for her own peace of mind. She kept thinking of his hands on her skin, and the way in which her body had responded to him. Was her memory playing tricks on her? Had she really never felt anything so pleasurable as that? Sophia considered herself a sophisticated woman, beyond being surprised, but Nicholas Blake had been a revelation.

She wriggled in her seat, feeling flushed and feverish. Would he be willing to do it again if she revealed she had been the masked woman? And was she really risking her peace of mind by considering such an insane gamble?

Webster knocked on the door, startling her out of her extremely inappropriate thoughts. "Your Grace, Mr. Blake is here. Should I see that supper is served?"

Sophia cleared her throat. To her relief her voice sounded normal. "Yes, thank you, Webster."

There was a small table set up by the fire in her favorite sitting room, and the intimate quality of it made her wonder if she should have chosen the long dining table with him seated at one end and she far away at the other.

Too late now.

She rose to her feet, and a moment later Blake entered the room.

He was solemn as he bowed politely before her. "Your Grace.

I appreciate you agreeing to see me." His gaze slid past her to the table by the fireplace and his mouth twitched, but he didn't quite smile.

Sophia ignored his look and gestured for him to be seated. There was a bottle of French red wine, decanted and ready to pour, and she filled his glass without asking, and then her own. She needed something to calm her nerves even if he did not.

"I am curious," she admitted at last. "What is so urgent that I must place myself once more in the dragon's den?"

He opened his mouth to answer but stopped when the food was carried in and served. Sophia kept to the usual topics, barely aware of what she said. The weather, the latest *on dit* concerning the Prince of Wales, and so on—she was well practiced in social chitchat. Finally they were alone again, but it seemed Blake wasn't ready to explain himself yet, after all.

"How is your sister? Lady Lyndhurst?"

The last time Blake was in this room he had brought Sophia's sister Ellis to her. Ellis had been in grave danger, and through Blake's machinations the man who wanted to hurt her had been caught.

Sophia smiled. "She is well, and happy." She was pleased for Ellis, truly, and yet thinking of her sister and Owen smiling into each other's eyes at their wedding made her feel strangely hollow inside. Both of her sisters were now happily married, and although she was glad for them, it also gave Sophia a sense of being the odd one out.

"I am relieved to hear it." He set aside his glass in a firm manner. "I want to explain to you why I need your help," he now said bluntly. "You may say no, but I am hoping you will agree."

"Because you helped Ellis," she mused. Of course that was why he brought up the subject of her sister. "I am very grateful to you for what you did. We all are. I am prepared to listen to you."

He was watching her carefully. "Here is the situation. As I said last night, I need you to gain access to my friend, Sir Gordon Robinson. He refuses to listen to me, and I am concerned that he is keeping the sort of company that could be harmful. I'm sure I don't need to explain why I feel that way. You are well acquainted with Oldney's set."

She opened her mouth, but he held up his hand.

"Rest assured, I do not want you to rescue him or anything so dramatic—I can do that if necessary. All I am asking you to do is sound him out—use your eyes and ears—and then report back to me. Once I know the situation, I will decide if I need to act to protect him."

Report back to him? He made her sound like a spy. Sophia made a doubtful noise and took a sip of her wine. "You seem to believe I can just walk back into the set as if things are still the way they were before Oldney died. I'm certain you have more power over these men than I do, Mr. Blake."

"But you *know* these people. They will talk to you, share their secrets. You spent a great deal of time with them when Oldney was alive. You may even consider them friends."

Sophia had never considered any of them her friends. Not after the first few weeks of her marriage to Oldney, when her eyes had been well and truly opened. She tolerated them, and even then barely. "I would have thought you had plenty of spies to call on," she said evenly. "I have heard it said that if you want to know something, ask Nicholas Blake and he will find it out for you."

They also said that he was the man to ask if you wanted someone taken out of the game. Permanently. Sophia wasn't sure how true that was.

He was still speaking, explaining his thinking to her. "I doubt my objectives could be achieved with someone new stepping into that group. Their suspicions would be raised immediately, and by the time they could be persuaded to trust the newcomer—if they ever did—it would be too late to help Gordon. You must know this." Then, with a frown, "If you do not wish to help me then say so, Duchess, and I will leave you be."

"I have not said I won't help you," she said impatiently. "I am trying to make you understand that these men have never been my friends. They were Oldney's friends and I was his wife. That gave me a certain level of protection from them."

"They frighten you."

She looked up sharply. He was watching her closely now, reading her thoughts as they passed across her face, and it was unnerving. When had she ever shown her emotions so openly?

"Yes, they do. I don't let them see it, though—that would be the worst thing I could do. If they scented for one moment that I was afraid, they would tear me apart."

He didn't look happy about that. "Tell me about them," he said gruffly.

Sophia took a breath. "Of the three, the Marquess of Chatham is the most dangerous. He comes from old money, but I'm sure he has little of it left. Lord Butcher is wed to an heiress, poor girl, and he thinks that by aligning himself with Chatham he is somehow made more important. Chatham borrows from him regularly. The third player is Sir Tomas Arnold who likes to pretend he is to be trusted, but I never have. Chatham is cruel and debauched, while Butcher is a fool, but not a particularly vicious one. Arnold likes to sit on the fence if he feels threatened. Out of them all, it is Chatham I would not wish to face alone in a room, but I believe I could manage the other two. When I was part of their set, I noticed how they all seemed to dislike each other, despite saying they were friends, and yet if anyone else spoke ill of them they would join together in destroying that person. They protect each other, would stand shoulder to shoulder against the world. You must understand, Mr. Blake, that being part of a group like that may be dangerous, but it is seductive. I imagine that is how your friend feels right now."

He said nothing, watching her sternly.

"Or perhaps I am expressing myself awkwardly," Sophia said lightly, and sipped her wine.

The fire was warm and she was replete, but she was anything but sleepy. Talking about these matters with Nicholas Blake had made her feel out of sorts and surprisingly vulnerable. The idea of being with those men again . . . In truth she wasn't sure she could do it, even for a good cause.

"This is a bad idea," he said abruptly, taking the words out of her mouth. "I should not have asked it of you. I will find another way of rescuing my young friend from their clutches."

Sophia wanted to agree that it was a bad idea, but in her heart she knew she couldn't refuse to help him. She was afraid, yes, but she could not let that stop her, and he deserved to know why. "Oldney behaved in a way that I ignored at the time, because I was powerless. As a young bride I was shocked, but I was also vulnerable. Now he is gone, I am remembering as if from a distance, but that doesn't make the things he did—the things any of them did—sit any easier in my conscience. I won't turn my back on what has happened. Not any longer. And helping you to save this young man would go some way to easing my guilt at remaining silent at the time. So my answer is yes, Mr. Blake, I will help you if I can."

He didn't seem to know what to say. His hand lay on the table, fingers restlessly tapping, and she suddenly had an image of that hand between her legs, his thumb circling her until she shattered. Was she blushing? She hid her face by bending it over the glass again.

"Very well," he said at last. "You construct a good argument. But if you feel unsafe at any time, you will walk away. Report back to me, and I will deal with the situation. Do you understand, Your Grace? Under no circumstances are you to risk your own safety."

He was so grave, she almost smiled. "Should I report to you at the houses of Parliament? Like your other spies?"

His lips twitched. "You have a romantic view of me, Duchess. You could send a message to me at my rooms in Edith Street, but there will probably be no need. I will be watching you when you meet with Chatham and his friends. Simply send me the time and the place, so I can be available."

Did that make her feel worse or better? Before she could decide, he rose to his feet and so did Sophia. He held out his hand and when she placed hers in it, he bent to set his lips against her skin. She looked down at his dark head, his hair neatly cut, and saw a couple of stray gray hairs mixed in with the ebony. He was a man only in his early thirties, so it surprised her, and she was unprepared when he straightened and said quietly, "Honeysuckle. My favorite perfume."

She was still standing there when the door closed behind him.

Sophia felt as if her head was spinning. The memory of their tryst at Vauxhall was suddenly so clear. Had he remembered it, too? But surely if he had remembered he would have said something before now? She reminded herself she had been in disguise. Her secret was safe and this was a coincidence, that was all. It must be.

Chapter Four

NICHOLAS CURSED SOFTLY to himself as the door to the townhouse in Berkeley Square closed behind him. He shouldn't have said that. Why had he? Because just for a moment, her closeness, her scent, had made him lose concentration, and now she would be wondering if he realized she had been the woman that night at the Vauxhall Pleasure Gardens. She would be remembering her gasps and his moans, her body clenching hard on his cock at the last until he thought he had died and gone to heaven.

What if she refused to help him now that she knew?

He had not forgotten that night and, judging by the shocked expression on her beautiful face, neither had she. He could play dumb, but he rather thought the cat was out of the bag now, and there was no putting it back in.

At the same time, he wondered if she regretted their moments together. It was certainly the opposite for him. That night was one he revisited regularly in his memories, and it never failed to stoke his passion and soothe his turbulent soul.

Nicholas knew he led a dangerous life, and it was not one he had ever wished to share. He had no wife or mistress, no children, and no happy home to return to when his day was done. His enemies were always seeking ways to bring him down, so friendships and closer bonds were risky to any person involved. Sexual comfort was also not something he took for granted, and he rarely visited the same place twice. So many times when Nicholas sought out female companionship, driven by his need for the touch and warmth of another body, he was left unsatisfied.

But when he had found himself at Vauxhall Gardens on another matter and caught sight of Sophia, he had made an uncharacteristically snap decision to indulge in a moment of her company. He had thought only to dance with her, nothing more.

She was someone he had paid a great deal of attention to over the years. Not just her place in the *ton* and her past, but little things like the manner in which she turned her head, the dark gloss of a curl of her hair lying against her cheek, the gleam of her brown eyes between her lashes. Even her voice, despite her only whispering, was familiar. He had recognized her easily, and if he had any doubts, as they walked down the secret paths in the garden, those doubts had dissolved when her perfume had filled his head. It was a scent he had always associated with Sophia.

Nicholas had long ago accepted that despite her enmity, or perhaps because of it, he greatly enjoyed their encounters. That spark of hatred in her eyes, the twist of dislike to every word she spoke. They crossed swords whenever they met, and whenever he bested her he felt particularly smug. And when she bested him . . . it made him secretly smile. He wasn't sure why their animosity was so exciting to him, but he wondered if it was the same for her. Sometimes their clashes felt like a courtship rather than a conflict.

That night in the gardens, when he had held her in his arms, when he had buried himself deep inside her and heard her cries of pleasure, he had known the memories would live with him forever.

Now he had seen another side to her, an unexpected but pleasing one. When he had told her about Gordon, she had paid attention, and he could see her concern for his friend. She understood why he wanted to save Gordon, and he thought she might even concur with his heroic endeavors. And dash it, then she had agreed to help him, and all he could think was that she was putting herself in danger.

Nicholas would need to keep a close watch on matters. Particularly on Chatham, that vile aristocrat who, now that Oldney was gone, seemed to be running the show. His thoughts strayed again to Sophia, and he wondered if she had ever been hurt by any of them, but he decided not. Not physically, anyway. Oldney was possessive of her, and he would have made certain she was protected from Chatham and the others. Of course, that did not mean Oldney had not hurt her himself—Nicholas would not have put anything past him. He had wanted to ask her, but he had bitten back the impulse, knowing she would not appreciate his stepping outside the boundaries of their acquaintanceship.

When Nicholas reached home—his spartan rooms in Edith Street—he flung himself down in the chair by the fire and took a deep breath. His landlady had left a plate warming on the hearth and he reminded himself to thank her. If it weren't for Mr. and Mrs. Shirley, he probably wouldn't have bothered to eat. Often, he was too weary or too sickened by what he saw about him to have an appetite. Nicholas had glimpsed the best and worst of humanity during his years as a man for hire.

If you were in a fix, then he was the one to call.

Recently, he had been seeking some agitators who had been bent on inciting rebellion against the government, but they were so inept their plot would never have worked. All the same, there was relief around Westminster when he delivered the fellows, and he was paid a nice sum for his work. He lived simply, so he also had savings, money set aside for a rainy day, money he rarely touched. But now he asked himself: Would that day ever come? And how could it when there was one vital question he still hadn't found the answer to?

His younger sister, Fern, had been missing for more than ten years now. It was her disappearance at the age of seventeen that had been the catalyst for Nicholas to begin his line of work, and in between that work he had searched relentlessly for Fern. His father still believed that against all the odds his son would find her. If he stopped looking . . . How could he disappoint the man who had been everything to him since his mother had died shortly after his sister was born?

Reverend Blake was a minister at an exclusive private school for boys, and because of his father's privileged position, Nicholas had also attended the school. He had not enjoyed being the butt of jokes and bullying from the more affluent and sometimes titled boys, but he had been able to hold his own. His sister had taken lessons, too, but privately, and once she was older she spent her days helping in the kitchen, or sitting with the boys who were in the infirmary and cheered them up by reading them stories and playing games. She was an angel, and everyone loved her, and then one day she was simply gone. There had been an investigation, but an unsatisfactory one, in Nicholas's estimation. Eventually, the school had bowed to Nicholas's demands, and questioned the boys, the staff, and anyone else he could think of. And yet no one had been able to solve the mystery of his sister's disappearance.

That was ten long years ago, and the reverend had retired to a cottage on the grounds, although he still took on the role of religious adviser when asked. Like his daughter, he was universally loved, but although he accepted most things as God's will, he could not come to terms with the loss of his daughter. Instead, he put his faith in Nicholas's ability to find Fern, to restore her to her family, and he had never lost the belief that one day, Nicholas would succeed.

When Nicholas was having a bad day, his father's faith in him was more of a burden than a matter of pride, and one he almost wished he did not have to bear.

He shook his head wearily. There was still a spark of hope he could find Fern, but with every year that passed it grew dimmer. And even if he could convince himself to walk away from this life and this task, what would he do? He doubted there was some rose-colored future awaiting him when he carried the guilt of failure. The best he could do was sit on a mountain top somewhere, alone, and watch the sun rise and set.

The loss of Fern made his rescue of Gordon, the young fool, from his own stupidity so vital. He couldn't face another failure.

When Gordon had been a child, he had followed Nicholas about like a puppy, and gazed up at him as if he were brighter than the sun. The boy had been miserable at the exclusive school, and the minister had suggested Nicholas take him under his wing. It had worked for them both—Nicholas had been miserable, too. He had never fit in with the wealthy, privileged boys who were his classmates. He had come to view Gordon almost as a younger brother, and they had formed a bond he had thought was unbreakable. Until now.

Nicholas considered again Sophia's descriptions of the three men, Chatham, Butcher and Arnold. She was afraid of them, but she was willing to go into the lion's den for Gordon's sake. She was brave as well as beautiful, but he would not allow her to be injured by joining forces with him in his loyal and perhaps misguided effort to save someone who did not want to be saved.

He wasn't sure whether he and Sophia were still enemies, but if she was hurt in all this . . . well, Nicholas would never forgive himself.

Chapter Five

OVER THE PAST week Sophia had visited her modiste twice and taken possession of some rather lovely new gowns. She was wearing one now, a dark-blue silk with long sleeves and the currently fashionably short bodice that was designed to show rather a lot of bosom. She had considered using a chemisette for a more modest look, but decided her charms might be a useful distraction while she questioned Oldney's friends.

Some cautious inquiries had revealed that Oldney's friends were to be found at Hettie Devenish's gambling establishment most nights of the week.

She had ordered the coach to her front door and was about to descend the steps to the driveway when suddenly a woman appeared out of the shadows in front of her. She wore no cloak and no bonnet, and the wind whipping around the square was not kind this evening. Sophia's first thought was that the poor thing must be frozen.

"Your Grace?"

Startled, Sophia stared down into a face that, in the shadows thrown by the flaring torch in its sconce, looked worn and weary. A gust of wind made the flame flare, and the woman startled, eyes wide. Where had she come from? Had she been hiding here in the shrubs until Sophia appeared? And more importantly, what on earth was she doing here?

Sophia asked cooly, "Who are you? I do not have time to speak now, I have an engagement to attend."

It was the sort of tone that usually sent people scurrying, but the woman did not move, as if she had built herself up for this moment and was determined to see it through.

"No, you do not know me. My name is Marianne. I am . . . I *was* your husband's mistress."

Sophia was momentarily speechless. She had known there must be other women—men like Oldney always had other women. She had been relieved that she had never heard anything of them and could therefore pretend they did not exist, more from a sense of humiliation than because she cared that Oldney was sharing his favors. She was still his wife, his duchess, and therefore she deserved at least that much consideration.

"Congratulations," she said stiffly. "Now, if you will excuse me, I really must go."

The woman, Marianne, did not move. "I am very sorry to burden you with my troubles, but since Oldney died I have been barely surviving. And the child needs food and shelter. I wondered . . . I hoped that perhaps you would find it in your heart . . ."

Was this actually happening? Sophia had never heard of such a thing. She was certain no one who knew her and called her "ice queen" would ever think her a soft touch. She opened her mouth to tell Marianne to leave and instead heard herself say, "What child?"

Marianne visibly swallowed and lifted her chin higher. She was standing on the step below Sophia and seemed small because of it. Her arms were covered in a thin, long-sleeved spencer and her hands were without gloves. She must be very cold. Hadn't Oldney made provision for the woman? Although because his death had been sudden, Sophia thought he may not have had the chance.

She reminded herself that it was most definitely not her problem.

"He is eight," Marianne answered with a hitch in her voice. "His name is Hugo."

Sophia blinked. "That was Oldney's father."

"Yes. He asked for the child to be called after his father. He thought it a fine jest, but I did not mind. I was glad to please him. He was not, as you must know, Your Grace, an easy man to please."

He wasn't, but Sophia was damned if she was going to discuss him with this woman as if they were cozying up for a good gossip about *her* husband.

Behind her in the doorway, her butler spoke. "Madam? Is this *person* being a nuisance?"

Marianne jumped at the sound of his voice, and looked about her anxiously, as if afraid she was about to be seized and thrown out into the street. And that was exactly what would happen in most cases of this sort. That was what *should* happen now.

But suddenly Sophia felt a wave of weariness wash over her. She had been a widow for a year, alone in this big, empty house, and this woman looked half starved. What did it matter? Who cared if she offered her husband's mistress some small assistance? The gossips could say what they liked—they always had—and Sophia was tired of trying to please the *ton*. When Oldney was alive it had mattered. He would have made her pay if she'd ever caused the wrong sort of scandal. But now it did not.

"No, Webster, she is not a nuisance. In fact, I would like you to ask for a room to be prepared for her, and a hot meal."

She could see Webster stiffen in outrage. "Your Grace," he blustered, "I do not think . . ."

Sophia ignored him. It was Marianne's expression that held her attention now. Tears gleamed in the woman's eyes and her lips wobbled as if she was fighting to hold herself together.

"Your Grace . . ." she gasped.

"Where is your son?" Sophia asked sharply, wondering if the poor child was hidden in the bushes somewhere.

"With a friend," Marianne watched her as she said it, as if she didn't expect Sophia's largesse to extend as far as the child.

"Then you must collect him in the morning and bring him here."

"Your Grace!" Webster sounded outraged.

Sophia tried not to smile. It felt rather gratifying to have rattled her indefatigable butler into displaying some genuine emotion. "I have given you my instructions," she said, turning to him, "and now I must go. I will discuss anything further tomorrow, Webster. Is that understood?"

The butler seemed at a loss for words. Marianne was not.

"Thank you, Your—Your Grace," she said, her voice shaking. "I cannot . . . I wish I could . . . I am so grateful to you."

"Yes, well, we shall discuss that tomorrow, too."

And Sophia sailed past her and down the steps to the coach. Like Marianne, she felt shaken. Oldney's mistress, for goodness' sake! But she felt something else, too. Those same feelings she had experienced when she had agreed to help Nicholas Blake's friend. A warm flush of pleasure, a sense of the *rightness* of her action. Was this how do-gooders felt when they went about their charitable work?

She hoped it would not become addictive.

Chapter Six

HETTIE DEVENISH'S HOUSE was ablaze with lights, and laughter drifted from the doorway. Sophia made her way through the rooms of what had once been a private dwelling and was now a gambling house. Hettie, finding herself abandoned by her husband and in deep debt, had been desperate. But instead of selling up and retiring in poverty to the country, she had decided to open a hell. At first it was a curiosity. However, in the years that followed, it had become fashionable to be seen there and to play a game or two. These days, men and women flocked to her establishment, even the respectable members of society. Because they had once known Hettie socially, they felt comfortable in her company. Besides, there were large fellows on the door to repel undesirables.

It was a year since Sophia had been here, but nothing much seemed to have changed. Perhaps the covers on some of the chairs and the supper menu, but the rest was as before. Even the faces looked familiar. Hettie, pretty and plump, greeted her effusively, until, remembering at the last moment that Sophia was now a widow, she clutched her arm and leaned in close.

"My condolences, Duchess. I was sad to hear about . . . You must be . . ."

"Thank you, Hettie. I am of course devastated."

The two women exchanged a knowing look. "You are out of mourning," Hettie said, her gaze taking in the new gown. "Very nice, Your Grace. I am glad to see you have not faded away to a shadow."

"I am rather like you in that respect," Sophia said, enjoying the chance to converse with the perceptive woman. "I do not let circumstances get the better of me."

Hettie smiled. "I must say that opening this place was the best decision I ever made. Are you here to play? I have several ladies here tonight if you wish to join them."

"Thank you, but I am looking for Chatham."

Hettie's eyes widened, and she opened her mouth as if to ask questions or issue a warning, and then changed her mind. "I am sure you know your own business, Your Grace. He and his friends are in the pink room." Hettie pointed up the stairs. Then called after her, "Are you sure you won't join me at the Faro table?"

"No, thank you. Perhaps later."

The pink room was so called because of a large painting hung on one wall of a woman whose opulent curves were barely restrained by her pink gown. The tables and chairs were not as crowded in here as the other rooms, and there was even a sofa to rest upon. Sophia saw her quarry at once. The marquess and his two friends and a young handsome gentleman whose flushed face and bright eyes looked very much out of place in such jaded company.

Sir Gordon Robinson, she presumed. He appeared to be even younger than she had expected, his brown hair styled fashionably, his cravat carefully tied, and a glass beside him that looked almost full. As she watched, she saw Arnold lift the bottle to add to Robinson's glass only to frown.

"You are tardy tonight, Robinson," he complained. "Drink up."

The young man smiled and took a restrained sip. Sophia wondered if that was on purpose, to prevent his glass from being refilled too often. Perhaps Gordon wanted his wits about him. Or perhaps he wasn't much of a drinker of the watered-down wine Hettie Devenish served in her hell.

Chatham had glanced toward the door, and he started when he noticed her. "My dear Duchess!" he cried out in surprise, his usual drawl missing. He quickly smothered any emotion and rose languidly to make his bow. "How delightful to see you."

Sophia approached with a smile and accepted the chair he gestured for her to take beside him. "And you, Chatham. I have been incarcerated in my house for far too long, and tonight I was desperate for some company. And as luck would have it, here you all are!"

She beamed about at them, and if they were surprised by her excitement they hid it well behind smiles of their own.

The table before her was covered in cards, and it appeared from the pile of money in the center that there had been some deep play. She turned to the young man who sat opposite her. "You are new, sir. We have not been introduced."

The color rushed into his face. "I am—" he began but was interrupted.

"This is Sir Gordon Robinson," Chatham said. "Robinson, I'm sure you have heard us speak of the Duchess of Oldney."

"Although words can never do her justice," Lord Butcher said.

"Huh, still a flatterer, my lord," Sophia responded.

Chatham chose to lean in to her then, close to her ear. Too close. She tried not to stiffen and pull away, because she suspected he knew how much she disliked him and that was why he did it. "This dear boy has taken Oldney's place. Not that anyone could ever do that, of course. Oldney was irreplaceable."

There was a murmur of agreement, and Sophia said somberly, "He was."

"We miss him a great deal," Chatham added in that emotionless drawl, and yet as Sophia met his watchful blue eyes she believed him. He *did* miss Oldney; the two men had been bosom bows since their school days.

The others had now joined in, vying with each other to express how much they missed her husband, and she thanked them for their kindness. It was strange, but she almost expected the late duke to arrive and sit down beside her. It felt so much like old times. But they were all a year older, and Chatham especially looked as if that year had not done him any favors. He was of a similar age to Oldney, and his hair had grayed markedly, while there were new lines of debauchery carved into his once-handsome face. Lord Butcher was in his late thirties but wasn't wearing it well. He had a petulant twist to his mouth, his auburn hair cut severely short, and his belly had grown rounder from overindulgence at the dinner table. Sir Tomas Arnold, the youngest of the three, was pouring himself some more wine, and Sophia noticed his valet had missed a section of his jaw when he'd shaved. Unless Arnold had run out of funds and had had to turn off his valet again—it used to happen regularly.

Once they were all settled again, Sophia gave the newcomer a chilly smile. "Sir Gordon, I am surprised you are not with gentlemen your own age."

Another flush of color, but this time Robinson also looked annoyed. "I am twenty-five, Your Grace, and if you must know I am bored with gentlemen my own age. They are no fun."

The marquess squeezed the boy's shoulder. "We are honored to have him here."

But there was something so false in his expression, in his tone, that Sophia almost burst into laughter. It was obvious to her that young Sir Gordon had something these gentlemen wanted, and because she knew them so well, she guessed it was money. Chatham barely made ends meet, and she thought she remembered that Lord Butcher had recently been accused of spending his wife's dowry on horses. Sir Tomas Arnold was more of a mystery, but over the years his fortunes, too, had waxed and waned.

She did not join their game in progress but watched as it

played out. Robinson lost, but he seemed good humored about it, especially when the others praised him for some clever play. "It won't be long before you are wiping the floor with us, my boy!" Chatham said, sounding almost jovial.

Sophia doubted it. Robinson was a flat, the perfect soft touch, and he was the only one who didn't know it.

"Have you been acquainted with these gentlemen for long?" she asked as the money was raked into the marquess's pocket.

"A few months," he said with a manic grin. "They are dashed good fellows."

A smile was passed around, and it wasn't a nice one. "Our young friend here has proven himself a courageous fellow," Sir Tomas said. "Butcher had an encounter with an angry husband last week and Robinson saw him off. Didn't you, lad?"

Gordon flushed again with pleasure. "Well, to be fair, sir, you helped," he said, but Sophia could see the boy was flattered enough to believe it was mostly his doing.

"The night is young," the marquess drawled. "We would love for you to join us, Duchess."

Sophia shook her head regretfully. "I have an unexpected guest, and I must get back."

It occurred to her then to mention Oldney's mistress, but at once she decided against it. These men would not be sympathetic to Marianne, and they would certainly not want Sophia to have anything to do with her. They might even accuse Marianne of being a liar. It was a further complication she didn't need at this time.

"Pity," Chatham said. "But we plan to visit Diablo's tomorrow night. It is a new hell that has recently opened. The play is deep but the company amusing. You *will* join us there, won't you?"

The others bowed to her as they rose. "It is almost as if Oldney is back with us again," Butcher said.

Chatham smiled politely and Arnold smirked. As they left and headed downstairs, Hettie Devenish was lingering beside the door and drew her aside, with a glance to make sure they were not overheard.

"I do not wish to speak out of turn, but . . . you've seen Robinson, Your Grace?"

"Indeed I have."

Hettie raised her brows. "He is going to be taken advantage of. Damaged. You need to keep an eye on him."

Sophia hesitated, but she knew Hettie would not gossip. They had known each other for years. "He is the reason I am here."

Outside, her coach was waiting for her, and still deep in thought she stepped into it. She had barely settled herself in her seat as the vehicle moved forward, the horses clip clopping over the cobbles.

"How did it go?"

The voice, coming out of the shadows, made her jump violently and she let out a squeak. The intruder moved, so that the light from the coach lantern fell on his face, and she was both relieved and disturbed to see it was Nicholas Blake.

Sophia tried to catch her breath, her hand to her breast, beneath which her heart was pounding. Being in the company of those men had made her jumpier than she would otherwise have been. She had had to be on her guard the whole time, and Blake's sudden appearance just as she had thought herself able to relax had discombobulated her. And what was he doing here?

"Did I ask you into my coach?" she demanded sharply. "I'm sure I would have remembered if I had."

His dark eyes shone in the lamplight. "I was hardly going to allow you to enter that dragon's den without protection, not once you sent me word you would be here tonight." He said it as if the answer was obvious.

"*Allow me?*" she repeated in disbelief. "You were the one asking me for a favor."

He appeared to consider several replies before discarding them, and when he spoke he ignored what had gone before. "And did you find out how Gordon is faring?"

He really was the most infuriating man. Sophia took a breath and strove to hold back her temper. "He is well entrenched with them, and they are very happy to have him there. Tell me, Blake, is he wealthy? Does he have relatives who may be of use to desperate men? Because I do not believe they are ensnaring him in their group for the sake of his blushes and his pretty smile."

As he listened, she could see his features hardening. "He is very wealthy, yes, and has full access to the family coffers since his father died. His father was already one of the richest men in the country when he married his mother, also from a prominent family. I don't know a great deal about his other relatives."

"What of you?" Sophia asked curiously. "Could he call upon you for a favor, and would you grant it to him, even if it were outside the law?"

Nicholas frowned. "That is a clever idea, Duchess. I will give it some thought."

Sophia yawned. "Now that I have done as you asked," she said wearily, "can I withdraw from this unpleasant game?"

He seemed perplexed. "I am assuming you are jesting. Assessing his situation has only just begun. I want you to keep an eye on the boy. If I need to act swiftly, it will be at your say so."

The truth was she was relieved not to bow out, although she wasn't going to tell him that. She was concerned for Sir Gordon, and she felt that same do-gooder urge as before, to save him. Not that she was going to tell the man opposite her *that* either.

"But what do *I* get out of this little charade? Apart from late nights that interfere with my beauty sleep." She chose the words that would irritate him the most.

He smiled, damn him. "Your beauty is unchanged, but if you want a reason to behave like a good citizen then you should consider this a way to right the wrongs your husband was guilty of. You might be losing sleep, but you can wake up in the morning and feel good about yourself."

She curled her lip. "You, sir, are an arrogant prick."

His eyes flared, but his grin was unrepentant. "Ah-ah, that is not something a lady should say. But I am sure you have had a testy evening, so I will ignore your insult."

He really was infuriating. "Get out," she said between gritted teeth.

He laughed, and now she really was so angry it was as if there were a flame-red cloud of fury spinning in her head. It was rare that Sophia lost control, but she did now. She launched herself at him, her hands balled into fists. He caught her with a huff of laughter, which only made her angrier. He wrapped his strong arms around her struggling form, his breath warm against her cheek.

"Duchess, please . . . Sophia, stay calm . . ."

"I'll give you calm," she said. "I did what you asked, and instead of thanking me, you speak in that unutterably smug way. Those men . . . those men . . ." But she couldn't go on. Suddenly the fight went out of her, and she slumped against him. She thought he would let her go then, but he didn't.

"Sophia," he whispered, "I *am* grateful, I *do* thank you. And I apologize if you did not know that."

Her eyes were squeezed shut, but now she opened them and looked up at him. He was very close. She realized then that he was holding her so that she was on his lap, and her hair had come loose and was a dark tangle against his jacket. He ran the back of his hand down her cheek and paused to stroke his thumb over her lips.

The air began to fizz for an entirely different reason.

For a moment they stared into each other's eyes, and then abruptly he leaned forward until his mouth brushed hers. It might have begun as a gentle kiss, but it soon turned into something else entirely. And Sophia was helpless to stop it.

Chapter Seven

NICHOLAS HAD NO idea how their argument had turned into this. In some faraway part of his brain he knew he should stop. Move back. Distance himself. And he told himself he would do that, just give him a moment more, just a little longer . . .

Her warm, sweet mouth opened to his, and he groaned as his tongue explored. Her gown rustled as she pressed against him, and then she was straddling his thighs, and his hands were pushing up her skirts and her bare skin was beneath his palms.

A delightful amount of it.

She wasn't stopping and neither was he, and it felt as if he had been waiting for this moment since their meeting at Vauxhall Pleasure Gardens three months ago. And now it was here he wasn't about to let it slip away through some mistaken belief in propriety, in the idea that he was a gentleman and she was a lady. Because right now neither was true.

Her warm hands were tugging at his shirt, and then they were beneath it, sliding over bare skin, while he had her indecently low bodice tugged down and his mouth was on her breasts. She grasped his shoulders, her fingers digging into him, while he lathed her with his tongue, sucking at the tips until she arched and made sounds of delight.

"I want you," he said it clearly, in case she needed convincing.

"Yes," she whispered, her mouth against his jaw, his throat. She sucked at his skin, and he knew there would be a mark. She probably did it on purpose.

His hands were back beneath her skirts, gripping her hips, squeezing the globes of her bottom. Her fingers were fumbling at the buttons of his breeches, opening them, delving inside, and . . . He groaned so loud he suspected the horses might take fright. He felt her shake with laughter, but it was only for a moment and then he was pressing his palm between her legs and the moist heat spoke of her desperate need.

He paused to look at her. Her hair was a tangle and her cheeks were flushed, her eyes almost wild as she wriggled closer, eager for him to take her. Nicholas lifted her and . . . How he got inside her he didn't really know, but here he was, and as he pushed deep they both groaned. And then he was moving and she was, too, and it was a race to the finish. In the end, they both won, coming within seconds of each other. After that the ripples of pleasure held them silent, satisfied in a way he could never remember being before.

Everything slowed down, and there was nothing important enough to send him rushing off. He wanted to stay here, holding her in his arms, forever.

She was lying heavily against him, the shape of her body melded to his, her cheek resting against his shoulder, and he bent his head and pressed his lips to the top of her head. It felt perfect and he didn't want to go anywhere, but at the same time he was aware that he would need to, before the coach reached its destination.

It was Sophia who eventually moved. She pushed away from him, back to her own side of the vehicle, and he saw that she was disheveled to a marked degree. She began to right herself, tucking her hair back where it had escaped its pins and shaking out her skirts. She found her cloak and pulled it around her, lifting the hood over her head before she peered up at him from its shadows.

"That wasn't supposed to happen," she said huskily.

He chuckled as he tidied himself up and reminded her, "It has happened before."

She stared at him, and then sighed. "You knew it was me all along, didn't you?"

"At Vauxhall? Yes."

"And yet you said nothing."

"If I had said anything we wouldn't have enjoyed that memorable encounter."

Her mouth twisted. "How *did* you know?"

"At first? Your eyes and your mannerisms, the way you walked and danced. Your perfume was the final touch, but even so I was unlikely to mistake you for someone else."

"I knew it was you, too," she said at last. "As soon as I saw you. It seemed a fine joke to pretend I was a stranger."

The joke was on her, Nicholas thought, but did not say so. Was there a reason why they both recognized the other and both said nothing? He wondered if it was because it gave them the opportunity to behave in the manner they had been longing to behave but never could. The tension between them had been building over the years, and at Vauxhall it came to a head.

The coach began to slow. He wondered if she would ask him to come inside and take him to her bed so they could repeat the performance. He wanted that, he could hardly believe how much, but he already knew she wasn't going to. Although there was something very real between them, a frisson of passion that burned brighter each time they kissed, they weren't friends, or even lovers. They were a couple of lonely strangers taking advantage of an opportunity to fuck.

There, he had admitted it. He was lonely. He had been lonely for a very long time. Was Sophia the answer? Doubtful. Once this business with Gordon was over with, she would get on with her life and he would continue with his.

Nicholas must remind himself of that. He must put some distance between them before he made a fool of himself.

"When do you meet with Chatham and the others again?" he asked briskly as the coach drew to a stop in Berkeley Square.

She eyed him suspiciously a moment before answering in an equally sharp tone. "Chatham mentioned that they would be at a hell called Diablo's tomorrow night."

"Diablo's?" His eyes narrowed. "A place that lives up to its name. Diablo's is not safe."

She scoffed. "I am not afraid. I could take a servant if I were anxious, but I am not. As you are aware, Blake, I am not the sort of lady who sits at home with her embroidery."

"I am aware," he murmured. "Won't they think it strange when you join them again so soon?"

She shrugged. "Why should they? I am now out of mourning, and I have told them how much I miss Oldney and how bored I am with my own company."

"And do you? Miss your husband?"

Sophia's dark eyes glittered. "I think that is a conversation for another time, Mr. Blake."

He didn't respond, although he would have dearly loved to know all of her secrets. He also had the urge to tell her to be careful, but he knew what she would think of that.

"Do you wish to go somewhere in my coach?" she said coolly into the silence. "I would hate for you to be assaulted by footpads."

He laughed. "Don't sound so dismayed at the thought, Duchess."

She smiled although he was certain she was trying hard not to.

Nicholas reached out to open the door and she stepped down. He jumped down beside her and bowed. "Good evening, Your Grace," he said.

"Good evening, Mr. Blake."

He spun about and began to walk across the square. He wasn't sure where he was going, but the fresh air was helpful in clearing his head. He only allowed himself to look back when he had reached the entrance into Curzon Street. She was no longer there, and he felt a foolish sense of disappointment that she wasn't gazing after him in some lovesick fashion.

Well, of course she wasn't. And she probably wasn't missing him already either, as he was missing her. Nicholas rather suspected he was developing a tendre for Sophia, and that was not good. Not good at all. He would need to put a stop to it.

He would do that—after he had rescued Gordon and seen Sophia safely out of the reach of those vicious men.

Chapter Eight

ONCE SHE WAS inside, Sophia gave a sigh of relief. Her body was still humming from their brief, passionate tryst in the coach, and there was a warm ache between her thighs that she remembered from the last time. How was it possible to loathe someone and at the same time crave them? To want to push them away and at the same time desire their lips and their hands and their . . .

Well, she couldn't think about it right now. It was too confusing, and she was weary from an evening where she had been acting a part she no longer wanted to play. She could stop, of course she could, but her conscience wouldn't let her. After all these years of turning a blind eye to Oldney and his friends and their behavior, she was desperate to make reparation. Nicholas Blake was right in that at least.

It was strange, but she had thought he was contemptuous of her, believing the worst. Now it seemed she was wrong. Or was she? Whatever disdain he felt for her it hadn't stopped him tonight, although to be fair, it hadn't stopped her either. And now, after all that emotion and the pleasurable explosion of feeling at the end of it, she felt emotionally raw.

Stripped bare of more than her clothing.

When she had married Oldney and had taken her place in the

ton, she had spent a wretched first few weeks wondering what on earth she was to do. It was too late not to marry him—that had been done—so all there was left was to make herself into the wife he expected her to be in the hope of avoiding a measure of the misery that was to be hers. In time she had learned to wear a mask and hide her feelings so well that she had begun to wonder if she had any. She had not realized it then, but having molded herself so completely into the Duchess of Oldney, the real Sophia had almost completely vanished.

It was only since he had died that she had slowly begun to feel again, to be herself again, and tonight had shown her that she could actually feel too much. That mask she wore, that outer shell she hid behind, was beginning to crack. The real Sophia was peeping out, and the awful thing was she was not even sure who that Sophia was anymore. Was she an improvement over the old Sophia? She must be, mustn't she?

But being required to replace that brittle mask, to be the woman she knew she no longer wanted to be, was even more difficult than it had been the first time. And yet what choice had she if she was to save that stupid boy?

Webster was lurking in the hall, looking so uncomfortable that she stopped as she began to climb the stairs.

"Whatever is the matter, Webster? Have you eaten something that has disagreed with you?"

He stiffened as if he had a ramrod up his back and pursed his lips. "My apologies, Your Grace. I would never normally presume to question your instructions, but the person you invited into your house . . ."

"Marianne?" Sophia frowned. "What about her?"

He cleared his throat. "I think you are being taken advantage of, Your Grace. You have allowed this woman into your home, and I cannot remain silent on the matter."

"Do you know her?" Sophia said. "Did you ever see her with Oldney?"

He looked flushed, and his eyes darted away. "I did. She lived in Curzon Street, and he was able to walk to her lodgings."

"Good heavens," Sophia breathed. "And I never knew." Or rather, more truthfully, she hadn't wanted to know. "What happened to the place in Curzon Street?"

"Thatcher, your man of business, sold it and the money was returned to your coffers."

"Why wasn't I told?"

Webster cleared his throat again. "The duke left instructions. Although his passing was sudden, he was prepared. The woman was removed and the place sold."

So it wasn't just bad luck for Marianne that Oldney had died so suddenly. Had he always meant to callously wipe his hands of her? Sophia wondered what else she didn't know. "He left no provision for Marianne at all? Where was she supposed to go once the house was sold?"

Webster seemed surprised that she should concern herself with such matters. "That I do not know, Your Grace. I *believe* that the Marquess of Chatham was aware of this person. Perhaps he was supposed to take her in."

Sophia tried not to shudder. Had Marianne been passed around Oldney's set like a pouch of snuff? She opened her mouth to ask more questions and then changed her mind. She would speak to Marianne tomorrow—there was a story to be told, and she needed to hear it from the person herself.

"Thank you, Webster." Dismissed, her butler gave a relieved bow.

Sophia climbed the stairs to her rooms. She was even more weary now and the warm tingle from her encounter with Nicholas Blake had faded. She felt a little grubby—not from Nicholas, but from Oldney and his secret life and her time spent at Hettie Devenish's. She needed a bath to wash away the grime that clung to her, even if it was invisible to the eye.

Her maid was waiting for her, and Sophia ordered her bath, despite the late hour. She didn't feel guilty about waking servants; hers were well paid and better cared for than many others. As she lay back in the scented water, she closed her eyes and let her mind drift to that moment in the coach when Nicholas had kissed her. Such passion was new to her. She had never felt like that before, but then she only had Oldney for reference when it came to sexual relations.

He had been a practiced lover, and she had felt pleasure with him, but it was a mechanical kind of pleasure. She soon realized he did not feel for her beyond the need to display his prowess. Sophia had longed to fall into their encounters, to lose herself in his touch and allow her emotions to carry her beyond the physical. She remembered opening her eyes in the throes of their love making, only to find him observing her in a way that left her cold. There had been something machine-like about his caresses, his kisses, as if her climax was a prize for his efforts rather than a pleasure for them both. That emotional joining of two people that Sophia had wanted to feel at that moment was not reciprocated. She was on her own, a puppet to Oldney's puppet master.

It had begun to feel awkward, and when the novelty of their marriage had worn off and he no longer came to her bed, Sophia was relieved. He had mistresses, of course—she knew that, even if she never mentioned to it—and she had turned a blind eye like any good wife. Her bed may have been lonely, but at least she'd not needed not pretend it had ever been, or could ever be, anything else.

Sophia splashed some water, which was cooling now, and wondered how long she had been seated here, ruminating. Her marriage had been a matter of business, nothing more, like most Society marriages. She had come from a poor family, her mother the widow of a curate with three beautiful daughters, who had launched them upon the London scene in the hope they would marry well. They married better than she could ever have imagined, and when she declared that only dukes would do, even that came true.

Sophia had been giddy with excitement when she first arrived in London. It was everything she had dreamed of and more.

Oldney had begun paying his addresses early in her first season, and despite him not being the handsome young gentleman every girl wanted to marry, she had balanced the man against what he could offer and was content. Wealth and prestige were enough, or at least she had thought so at the time.

Sophia's sisters had also suffered in their marriages, but they had both been widowed earlier than she and had now found a different sort of life, one with love and happiness at the forefront. When she was in their company, Sophia could not help but wonder if she needed to be lonely in this big house. Yes, marriage could be a business arrangement, but couldn't it be more? Surely she could find someone this time who wanted her for more than the prize of her face, or now perhaps for more than her coronet and her money? But then again, why marry at all? She could take a lover who would come to her whenever she wanted him. A man who didn't care about *what* she was, but *who* she was.

Did such a man even exist? Irritably, Sophia splashed some more water and leaned back into the bath with a sigh. Unbidden, her mind returned to the coach. Should she allow herself another encounter like that? An opportunity would present itself with him trailing her across town, she was certain. He even knew she would be at Diablo's tomorrow night.

Her mood soured as she remembered who she would be meeting there, but if she could be with Nicholas afterward . . . Suddenly she felt like a child who, after taking a spoonful of nasty medicine, was offered a treat.

And Nicholas was that treat.

Chapter Nine

NICHOLAS SAT DOWN to Mrs. Shirley's hearty breakfast—a heaped plate of bacon, sausage, egg, and fried bread. Normally he would have demolished it within minutes. He was always hungry after a late, busy night, and last night had been busy indeed. Before he went searching for Sophia, he had located a group of jewel thieves who were planning to rob a leading member of the *ton*. Misguided rather than dangerous, but still better locked away so they could reconsider their futures.

It was another feather in his cap. He rarely failed when asked to complete a mission, and although he was not owned by any one person, his name was passed about as the man to call when there was trouble—and he was handsomely recompensed. His *real* job was a secret to everyone but himself and his father, and that was finding his sister Fern. She had lived in his memory now for ten years and he grieved for her.

When it happened, Nicholas had had little to go on. The school governors had not been helpful—they did not want any scandal like that attached to their institution. And anyway, what did the daughter of a reverend matter when their students were the sons of the wealthy and the titled? But Nicholas had been sure one of those boys must know something, and eventually he had struck gold. On the evening she had disappeared, Fern had been spotted in the lane outside the school gates with a small traveling bag on the ground beside her. It seemed as if she was waiting for a vehicle to collect her. When the young boy who saw her asked her where she was going she had laughed and said, "Why, London, of course!"

The boy had thought nothing of it at the time—and his fellows had suggested he not borrow trouble by coming forward once it was known Fern was missing—so it was not until several months later that Nicholas finally discovered him. By then her trail was cold, and despite extensive searching he had never found her.

There were still a great many unanswered questions.

Had she thought she would find a better life in the capital? A pot of gold at the end of the rainbow? He'd known that to happen to other young women. By the time they discovered London wasn't the castle in the sky they had imagined, they had become trapped in the cycle of poverty and desperation that resulted from their bad decisions. Was that what had happened to Fern? Had she simply been too ashamed to come home again?

Nicholas wished he could have spoken to her before she'd left. She had been seventeen then, and he had been nearly twenty-two, and by that time he was at university. He had pictured his life full of scholarly pursuits—perhaps he'd become a professor with cozy rooms in one of the colleges—but his sister's disappearance had changed all that. He had thrown aside his studies and become a hunter, searching for people who were missing, or as in the situation last night, who were hiding and dangerous. Nicholas was a man for hire and his job was lucrative enough to allow him to seek his missing sister in his spare time.

His father still believed Fern would be found, despite the years that had passed without new information. Only the other day he had written to Nicholas about a newspaper report of a child discovered in a forest, living with wild animals, as if Fern could have done the same. Nicholas had laughed aloud at the thought of his sister sitting down to dinner with badgers and foxes. And then he had wept, because the undertaking had begun to seem increasingly pointless. Some days he wanted to stop, but that would mean destroying his father's last hope, and Nicholas would not do that to him.

His thoughts drifted away from the ever-present seriousness of Fern and focused instead on a far more pleasant topic: last night with Sophia. It had been an agreeable diversion, and one he'd very much like to repeat. He had always thought about her far more often than he should. Over the years she had appeared regularly in his dreams at night, but now he daydreamed about her, too, and although he wasn't sure what that meant exactly, it worried him. He mustn't become obsessed with a woman who was never going to be around for longer than a few weeks. And yes, he was planning to keep an eye on her at the gambling hell she would be visiting with Chatham and the others, but that didn't mean he was lusting after her. She was doing him a favor with Gordon, so it was important to keep her safe.

Nicholas wouldn't be able to live with himself if anything happened to her, too.

He wasn't sure why it was Sophia who occupied his mind to the exclusion of the others whose company he had enjoyed over the years. He supposed because his work had always precluded anything more than a brief liaison, and those women had always faded away. Or perhaps he had allowed them to fade away because he wasn't as attached to them as he was Sophia, even as she had remained unreachable to him.

And even now that she was within his reach, he knew there would still come a day when she walked away, unless he walked first. Nicholas's head told him that would be for the best, but it didn't explain the ache in his heart.

DIABLO'S WAS A popular gambling spot for many of the wealthier members of the *ton*, as well as those in need of funds. The desperate could always be found lurking at the shoulders of the well-heeled. As with many of these hells, it was situated in a part of the city where there were plenty of drinking dens and brothels, a plethora of opportunities for pleasure. Women plied their wares along the narrow streets, and men circled around them.

As he passed, Nicholas cast a glance over the harlots, always looking for a glimpse of Fern, but none of the faces resembled hers. The thought that she may have ended up in such a place appalled him, but by now Nicholas had witnessed the fate of so many young girls, and he knew that Fern could easily be one of them.

He had dressed in sober clothing, so as not to stand out, and as he entered the hell, no one gave him more than a glance. He was good at blending in after years of practice. There was a small chance Gordon would see him and recognize him, but Nicholas was willing to take that chance. The risk to Sophia was greater. Now he made his way leisurely through the rooms, pretending to stop every now and again to inspect the play, while in truth he was looking for Sophia and the others.

He discovered them in a corner of the larger gaming room, at a cozy table behind a loud group playing Cassino. Nicholas found a seat against the opposite wall, half hidden behind the crowd, and slouched down as if he was half asleep or had over-imbibed on the surprisingly decent claret.

Chatham looked flushed, probably from the carafe of that same claret at his elbow, from which he seemed to be regularly refilling his glass. Butcher was frowning at his cards, his auburn hair sticking up as if he had been running his hands through it. Sir Tomas Arnold was watching Sophia in a manner that made Nicholas's blood boil. He would have liked to take the man by the scruff of his neck and toss him outside, but he gritted his teeth and stayed where he was. Gordon was giggling in a foolish manner, his eyes shining as he lost hand after hand.

The idiot.

Nicholas's gaze moved back to Sophia. She was smiling as she added to the play, and when she spoke, the others would guffaw or smirk, although Arnold just stared. Despite her earlier objections, she appeared to be enjoying herself. Was this task not as onerous as she had claimed? A niggle of doubt began to swirl like a poisonous mist in his head. Was she really to be trusted? Was he being gulled into thinking her someone she was not? Nicholas was no fool, but then again he had never been as captivated by a woman as he was by this one. What if it had fogged his common sense?

Just at that moment, she looked up and their eyes met. It was only briefly, but her smile seemed to freeze on her beautiful face before she quickly turned back to the others, laughing at something Gordon had said. Chatham slapped him on the back and Gordon flushed with pleasure.

Nicholas stood up and slid behind a group of noisy gentlemen who were in the process of leaving and made his way closer to the door. He should go. There was nothing to keep him here. Sophia had no need of him—she was obviously in her element—and the last thing she would want was for him to play some sort of guardian angel role.

And yet he couldn't seem to drag himself away.

Elegantly, she rose to her feet. She was wearing a blue gown tonight, but it had the same low-cut bodice, with only a scrap of lace to make it decent. He paused to watch her comment to the others, before she left the table and made her way toward the door. She walked right past where he was slouched against a wall, and he heard her murmur, "Follow me," without once looking at him. With one cautious eye on the others, who were still seated, Nicholas followed her.

An antechamber led off a second room where women and men seemed more interested in each other than gambling. Sophia was waiting for him, alone, staring into the fireplace. Nicholas had barely taken a step inside when she turned to face him, her skirts rustling and her dark eyes glittering.

"What are you doing here?" she hissed. Her cheeks were rouged while her bosom rose and fell with each quick breath she took. She might have been dressed appropriately for the hell, but Nicholas didn't like it one bit—he didn't like any of this. Her behavior confused him, and at the same time he wanted to carry her out of here to somewhere safe.

"Why shouldn't I be here?"

He sounded belligerent and he knew it. He had meant to tell her how he was keeping an eye on her because he was worried, that this was a dangerous place and she was involved in a dangerous game. He had meant to say that he was having second thoughts and she should go home and leave Gordon to his fate. But her combative attitude put his back up, and as always when it came to the duchess, he lost his temper.

She was still abusing him. "You wanted me to do this, and I am doing it. Go away. They will see you, and then it will all have been for nothing."

He strolled closer while she glared at him.

"You seem to be enjoying yourself for someone doing something she claims to hate." He could hear the accusing tone in his own voice.

Her eyes flared and she clenched her hands into fists at her sides. "Enjoying it?" she repeated, each word forced from between her lips. "I had not thought you such a fool, Blake."

"I am not considered one. Perhaps I speak the truth, and you don't want to hear it. You have been in mourning a year, and you must miss your old life. It would be understandable if you did." Now that he had made her angry, Nicholas felt surprisingly calm. "When you are laughing and sharing wine with your companions, talking over old times, then there is only one conclusion to be drawn, Duchess."

She stared back at him. He could see she was struggling to regain her own composure as she took one shaky breath and then another. Her eyes, brilliant with rage a moment ago, had lost their spark, and her mouth turned down. Suddenly her face was wan and rather bleak.

"And how else would you have me gain their confidence? Those men you speak of are not my friends, as I have told you before. They never were. They are despicable creatures, and I am only with them because I want to help *your* friend escape their grasp. And because . . ." she took another shuddering breath, "you were right. I feel I owe it to all the other victims I couldn't help to rescue him before it is too late. I have seen far too many willing fools and innocents fall for their lies and be sucked into situations from which they can never recover. I did nothing then, but I can now."

She was completely sincere. With a sinking heart he realized he had misjudged her. *Again.* He was embarrassed to admit why that was—he was jealous. It was the worst of reasons. Now he must grovel and beg her forgiveness.

"My apologies," he said. He took a step closer, until there was barely an inch between them. "I am in the wrong, Sophia."

"Then perhaps you should learn from your mistakes," she said, turning away. He moved at the same time, reaching out to stop her, and the button on his jacket sleeve snagged on the comb in her hair. Dark locks tumbled down in waves about her shoulders.

"Now look what you've done!" she cried.

There was a looking glass on the wall, and she went to it, attempting to repair the damage. Nicholas followed her, deftly catching up the long strands of hair between his fingers. The locks were heavy and soft, and her honeysuckle scent drifted around him.

"Let me," he said quietly.

Their eyes met in the mirror, and she looked as if she might refuse. "What, are you a lady's maid now?" she said impatiently.

He was already busily replacing the comb, looping her hair into its original style. "In a way I suppose I am," he admitted with a wry grin. Again he met her gaze in the mirror and suddenly the words spilled out of him.

"I had a younger sister whose hair was very untidy. Some mornings it was like a bird's nest. There were just the two of us—our mother died young and our father was always busy—so from an early age it was my job to make her look presentable."

"Nicholas, you're pulling!"

"There are knots, Fern! What sort of bird will I find in there this morning?"

Her giggle echoed down through the years, and the memory felt bittersweet. His voice was a little hoarse when he said, "I loved my sister very much."

Sophia watched his reflection steadily, as if she was reading his thoughts. "Where is your sister now?"

He frowned. "I don't know," he admitted reluctantly. "I wasn't there when she left home, although I tried to find her. Later I discovered she had gone to London. I have been searching for her for ten years and I have never found her. I've failed."

She reached up to still his hands and when she turned he found he could not look away from her. There was something compelling in her gaze, and more than a trace of compassion.

"Is that why you prowl about London? You are looking for your sister? That seems like such a—"

"A waste of time?" he cut her short. "Yes, I expect it is."

She gave an impatient shake of her head. "I was going to say that seems like such a laudable thing to do. You have dedicated your life to finding her, haven't you?" And when he didn't argue—in fact his throat had closed up, "Nicholas, I am so very sorry."

What could he say? Then he noticed there was still one curl of hair that had not been restrained and he quickly slipped it beneath a hair pin. Satisfied, he stepped back. "There," he said. "As good as new."

Sophia reached up to touch her hair, and then she smiled. "Thank you."

He bowed, relieved she was done with questioning him. "My pleasure, Duchess."

But she was not finished with him yet.

"I understand now. Your sister's tragedy has shaped you and made you the man you are today. There are far more layers to you than I realized, Nicholas."

He read admiration in her expression, as well as sadness. It made a change from the dislike she had always shown him prior to Vauxhall. Before he could remind himself of where they were and the dangers nearby, Nicholas slid his arms about her and gathered her in. "I can't stop thinking about you," he admitted. "You are not helping my ability to sleep at night."

"You cannot blame me for that," she said, her lips so close they were almost touching his.

He wanted to kiss her. Desperately. He might have done so, but in the next instant she was pushing him away so hard that he stumbled against a chair.

"Oldney was right about you," she said in a clear, carrying voice. "You are a despicable creature, Blake."

He was too shocked and startled to reply, which was just as well because next moment a droll, drawling voice spoke behind him.

"Duchess, and . . . Mr. Blake, is it? How odd to find you here, Blake. I did not think Diablo's was quite your thing. Bit of a puritan really, aren't you?"

Nicholas felt his heart speed up, while at the same time his nerves cooled to a degree where he could turn and look the marquess in the eye without giving anything away. He was good at his job and this was why. But all the same, that was a near thing! Thank God for Sophia's quick thinking.

"How do you know what my thing is, Chatham? But now you mention it I could do with a bath, to wash off the filth of this place." A glance at Sophia found her watching him closely, but he was glad to see that she was giving nothing away apart from her usual distain. "I will bid you adieu, Madam."

She curled her lip. "Go, Mr. Blake. You are not wanted here."

As he walked off, his scalp prickled. Behind him their laughter rang out, making him think he was the butt of their joke.

It was an act, he reminded himself. The Dowager Duchess of Oldney was almost as good as Nicholas at playing a part. She was well able to take care of herself.

There was no reason for him to punch Chatham on the chin and lay him out on the colorful rug before the fireplace. There was no reason for him to take Sophia in his arms and carry her to safety.

And yet he wanted to.

Chapter Ten

"Y OU AND BLAKE," said the Marquess of Chatham. "Who'd have thought! Hardly up to your standards, is he, my sweet?"

Sophia gave him a cool look. "There is no 'me and Blake,' Chatham."

"Then what did he want?" Chatham asked, a watchful look in his blue eyes.

She gave an impatient shrug. "I wasn't listening to everything, but I think he waylaid me to warn me."

The marquess gave a startled laugh. "Warn you? About what?"

Sophia laughed back. "Well, what do you think? The company I am keeping. I'm not sure whether he is trying to save me, although why he should want to do that is a mystery. Perhaps he just wants me to dance to his tune. I told him I did not want to dance! Insufferable man."

The last sounded genuine because it was, and the marquess seemed to relax.

"Oldney hated him," he said, idly swinging the fob on his watch chain.

"So do I," Sophia replied, with a defiant lift of her chin.

Chatham's smile was the nearest thing she had ever seen to

evil. "Then you will be thrilled with my plan. You know he is a friend of Robinson's? He will be very sorry indeed when he hears of our young fool's downfall. And even more gratifying, there will be nothing he can do to restore Robinson's good name."

Sophia had to work hard to keep her mask in place. Beneath her cool exterior her heart was thumping and her hands were damp with perspiration. She pretended to gaze about her, as if she was bored, and then shrugged her shoulders. "*Is* Robinson his friend? I hadn't realized."

Chatham almost rubbed his hands together in glee. "Oh, yes. Boyhood friends. They were at school together, and Robinson idolized him. That just makes it more satisfying now that we have the boy. Believe me, we plan to see him completely and utterly ruined. I would love to see Blake's face when he finds out. What do you think, my dear Duchess?"

He was still watching her intently, but Sophia now had her disguise firmly in place. She grinned with delight. "Oh, that is just so . . . well done, Chatham. Can I be there when Blake finds out his protégé is doomed? When is it to happen?"

He smiled but shook his head.

"Although," Sophia paused, as if giving the matter some thought, "how exactly do you intend to ruin him? He is rich, I gather, else why would you be wasting your time on him? He has been spending a great deal of money at the gaming tables. And he cannot have a bottomless pit of funds to draw on. Are you sending him bankrupt?"

The marquess smiled again and the sight of it made Sophia go cold. She could feel the malevolence seeping out of him and onto her own skin, and like Nicholas she wanted to go home and take a bath to wash it away.

"Nothing so simple, Duchess, although he will certainly be lighter in the pocket when we are done with him. Our plan is to place him in a situation that, when it becomes known, will be extremely damaging for him. He will turn to Blake for help, and that is when the fun begins. Will Blake risk his own reputation to save the boy, or will he throw him to the wolves? Whatever choice he makes, Robinson will suffer and so will Blake."

Her skin tingled, and nausea swirled in her stomach. They must hate Nicholas a great deal to do this, to ruin his friend simply to get to him. It was deliberately calculated to cause the most pain, and would be executed with cold, vicious precision. But she still did not know what "it" was. Sophia waited for a few moments in the hope he would say more—to ask would be too dangerous right now and she did not want Chatham to become suspicious.

"That is something I look forward to," she said when the silence drew on. "Imagine Blake's face!" She grinned and gave a wriggle, like a silly debutante.

Chatham gave her an indulgent look and then reached for her hand and lifted it to his lips. She tried not to flinch. "It is my pleasure, Duchess."

Together they made their way back to the table, where Sophia sat for another excruciating hour. She joined in their nonsense, and she won and lost, but nothing of consequence. She was an astute player. She smiled and laughed, as if she couldn't be happier to be back with her late husband's set. Eventually, after an increasing number of smothered yawns and an apology, Sophia rose to her feet announcing she would see them again at Hettie Devenish's.

Gordon glanced up at her, but the befuddled expression he had been wearing all night was suddenly absent. Surprised, she looked at him more closely, but he was already back to slurring his words and playing badly. Was it her imagination? Perhaps she was not the only one here tonight in camouflage.

The memory of Chatham's words made her fear for Gordon, but she also feared for herself. She had always known Oldney's set were vindictive and cruel, but she was beginning to suspect they were worse than that. *Evil*. That word again, but it was the only one that fit.

Once Sophia was outside, she was able to let her true feelings wash over her. She felt raw again, her pretense stripped bare. The air was cold, and she gave a shiver, drawing her cloak tighter about her as she waited for her coach. This was not a civilized part of town, and she knew the shadows and the alleys hid all sorts of miscreants.

Her thoughts returned to her encounter with Nicholas earlier. He had been searching for his sister all these years, day after day, night after night, and never finding her. No wonder he was driven, she thought as she climbed into the coach and they set off for Berkeley Square. And he had been honest with her. He felt as if he had failed his sister.

She wanted to comfort him.

Sophia groaned softly to herself. She was not supposed to be caught up in Blake's personal business. And yet, after their passionate encounters, how could she not find herself drawn to him, both physically and emotionally? He wasn't the man she had thought him, and she found she wanted to know him better. They were working together to save Gordon, and apart from her attraction, or maybe because of it, they made a surprisingly good team.

Impatiently Sophia shook her head. None of that mattered. This was a brief interlude in her life, and soon Nicholas would be gone and she would be alone again. It wasn't as if she didn't have plans. She had two sisters she could visit and a mother she had not seen in ages. She did not have to remain here in this big echoing house.

For the first time since she arrived in the capital, Sophia was not looking forward to throwing herself into London's social whirl, was in fact looking forward to something quiet and peaceful. Something meaningful and far from the superficiality of her life before.

The coach came to a halt, and the footman handed her out. As she climbed the steps to her front door, Sophia's head was still full of everything that had happened and how she was going to save Gordon from his own stupidity.

A shadow beside the shrubbery moved.

She gasped and jumped, ready to fling herself at the front door, before she realized who it was.

"My apologies, Your Grace," Nicholas spoke formally, with a bow. As if they were meeting at one of the Season's grand balls.

Her heart was still pounding, but the fear had drained away, leaving her weak. "You are behaving ridiculously," she said, her tired voice husky. "Can't you arrange a visit during the day like anyone else? Well I'm sorry but right now I only want my bed, Mr. Blake. Alone," she added, in case he imagined otherwise.

He smiled. Did he think that funny?

"I would not want to keep you from your beauty sleep."

She turned to the door, hesitated, and then with a sigh turned back again. "Although I do have things to tell you . . ."

He cocked an eyebrow, and then followed her inside.

Chapter Eleven

THE ENTRANCE HALL was lit by a single lamp, and the house seemed suddenly so silent. Sophia had been lost in it while she was in mourning. Rattling around like a ghost in a place that no longer felt as if it was her own. Marianne was here now, but Sophia hadn't heard a peep out of her. She reminded herself that she still had to talk to the other woman. Her time since Marianne appeared on her doorstep had been taken up by other matters, but Sophia still had questions for her. Webster had informed her earlier that "the child" had arrived, but she hadn't asked for details. Her butler would be only too happy to add to his complaints and Sophia did not want to encourage him.

She turned to the waiting servant. "Bring us some coffee. We will be in the Yellow Room."

As she walked toward the sitting room, she wished she had taken Nicholas to the drawing room instead, which was large and imposing and always made her visitors a little nervous. The Yellow Room was far more comfortable and informal. But did she want Nicholas to feel comfortable? Then she reminded herself that he probably would not feel discomforted wherever he was because nothing seemed to intimidate Nicholas Blake.

Or nearly nothing.

Which brought her to the subject at hand.

She gestured for him to sit in an armchair opposite, while she made herself comfortable in the other. They stared across the small space at each other, and she found herself examining his features. Sophia could see that he was as tired as she, the weariness causing shadows like bruises under his eyes, while lines bracketed his mouth.

He had admitted he hadn't been sleeping and she was the reason. She was keeping him awake. Well, that was only fair, because thoughts of *him* were keeping *her* awake.

A footman brought a tray with coffee and cups, and what looked like a large fruit cake. Cook was very proud of her fruit cake, justifiably so, and produced it on every possible occasion. Seeing it now, Sophia realized how hungry she was, and placed two thick slices on the delicate plates, handing one to Nicholas, before biting into her own with relish. After demolishing half of it, she set it aside and sipped her coffee. She was feeling better, more alert, and ready to speak.

This time when she met Nicholas's gaze she smiled. "Perhaps Chatham catching us together like that was a good thing," she said. "He was most forthcoming when I assured him that my hatred for you had not dimmed."

Nicholas laughed, and despite his untidy dark hair and un-shaven jaw, her heart gave a little flutter.

Not now! Sophia gulped some more coffee to steady herself, before setting down her cup. "He has plans for your young friend."

Nicholas's smile faded, his dark eyes piercing as he searched hers. "Tell me."

Swiftly and precisely she repeated Chatham's words to him while he listened in sober silence. "I have yet to discover just what it is they will use to ruin him, but I will do my best to find out. You will be able to stop it?"

"I hope so." He looked very grave now. "You must take care, Sophia. These men—"

"They would not hurt me."

He shook his head in disbelief. "Of course they would! If they thought you might harm them, that you were a threat, they would not hesitate. Men like that have no scruples. You must be very, very careful, Sophia."

Was he right? Perhaps. But she couldn't think of that. If she started to fear for herself, she would not be able to do what was required of her, and she was determined to stop them from hurting Gordon.

The clock on the mantel chimed two o'clock in the morning and Sophia looked at it in surprise. No wonder she was tired! Over the past year she had kept early hours, rising with the sun, and enjoying the beginning of the day. She had forgotten how fresh and new the world was at that hour. While she was married to Oldney she had rarely seen the sun before noon.

Nicholas Blake rose to his feet. "I should go," he said gruffly. "I thank you, Duchess, for your help. It means a great deal to me—and to Gordon, the young fool, if only he knew."

She rose too. "I am glad. At least something good has come from this."

He hesitated and she waited, because he clearly had something to say. "I should not have doubted you tonight. My apologies again . . ."

She waved a dismissive hand.

"When I saw you so enjoying their company, so free with your smiles, I . . ." He grimaced. "I was jealous, to be honest."

Sophia's eyes widened. He had said that before, but it had been lost in the moment. "Jealous?"

"You seemed so at ease with them. You inhabit your place in this world so effortlessly, as if you were born to the role. As I am often reminded by my enemies, I am a commoner aping my betters."

Sophia tried to come to grips with what he was saying. Yes, she had heard Oldney say those things about him, but she had not realized how they had stung Nicholas. And if he was jealous . . . Surely that suggested he had some feelings for her other than simply being pleased that she was of use to him. And lust. Let them not forget about the lust that burned so bright between them whenever they were close.

"It is all an act," she said quietly, earnestly. "I learned to pretend very early in my marriage to Oldney. It was the only way I could survive."

His mouth twisted in a wry smile. "You were very good at pretending," he said. "Until now, I never imagined you were other than you seemed. You fooled me, and I am not easily fooled."

"That is a good thing then, because if I can fool you then Chatham and the others will be a doddle."

He huffed a laugh as he came toward her, standing close enough that she could feel the heat from his body. He was taller than she, but not uncomfortably so. She looked up into his face, admiring the strong jaw and straight nose, his dark eyes with their long lashes. He was a handsome man. Even when she had been hating him she had thought so, but there was more to him than good looks. He was a moral man who believed in doing what was right and fighting against what was wrong, and if sometimes his view was too rigid, then she found she could forgive him. Because she understood him now as she had not done before.

To her surprise, Sophia also found that she liked him. She was coming to enjoy their conversations as much as their sexual encounters.

Nicholas was looking at her, too. She wondered what *he* was thinking, but then she knew. With a soft groan he bent his head and captured her lips with his.

His mouth was firm and warm, and it only took a moment for her to be lost in the pleasure of his kiss. Yes, it was late and she was tired, but none of that mattered now. She could not send him away, not when she would lie awake for the rest of the night, her body aflame with need.

She took his hand in hers and began to lead him toward the door. He came easily, fingers tightening. Out into the entrance hall and up the stairs to the gallery, and then along the passageway that led to her suite. The duke and duchess's suites adjoined, but these days the duke's side stayed dark and empty.

As soon as the door was closed, he took her in his arms, kissing her again. For a time, they were lost in each other, but this was different from their other frantic couplings. There was no rush, and he undressed her slowly, as if she was a gift he wanted to take his time over, his mouth sliding over her naked skin as if discovering it for the first time.

"So beautiful," he breathed, cupping her breasts in his hands, watching the creamy flesh spill over. With a groan he leaned in and took one nipple in his mouth and then the other. She arched back in delight, clasping his shoulders, her desire growing hotter. But he still seemed in no hurry.

When he went to his knees before her, she watched, dazed, as he nuzzled against the dark curls between her thighs, and then his tongue licked the heated, moist flesh. Sophia gasped and pressed against him, her hands tugging at his hair, as her passion rose to dizzying heights. Release was so close she could almost touch it. She expected him to stop now, to take her to the bed and push himself into her, taking his pleasure as she reached hers.

But he didn't. He continued to lathe her swollen folds in a manner that was quite spectacularly good as she trembled and cried out, all her focus on that place he was giving so much attention. And then the wave crashed over her, and she lost all sense of time and place.

It was a minute or several later, and she was lying on the bed, gazing up at the canopy. She blinked, and looked about her, and found Nicholas. He was watching her with a smile that could only be described as smug.

She cleared her throat and sat up, propped on her elbows, her long dark hair cascading about her. She opened her mouth to ask him where he had learned such skills and then decided against it. She didn't want to hear about other women. Suddenly she knew she wanted him all to herself.

"Undress," she said, her voice husky. "I want to see all of you."

His eyes flared but he obeyed her easily enough. Some men did not like to be told what to do—Oldney had always had to be in charge—and Nicholas's easy acquiesce relaxed her. He reached for his cravat, untying the simple knot, and then shrugged off his jacket. His white shirt was next, tugged over his head, and tossed aside.

Sophia sat up properly now, her gaze traveling over his broad chest with its dark hair spanning his manly nipples. Her mouth watered. "And the rest," she said, lifting her gaze to his. He smirked, but there was something in his expression that made her think this was new to him too, obeying her orders, and he wasn't quite sure whether he enjoyed it or not. And yet the fact that he was willing to comply gave Sophia a frisson of excitement. To have such a man bow to her will . . .

He unbuttoned his pantaloons, pushing them over his hips and thighs to the floor, and tugging them off with his boots. He tripped and almost fell over, which made her bite her lip on laughter, but it was Nicholas who laughed first. Standing only in his drawers, he hesitated a moment, and then divested himself of them, too.

His cock was hard, pointing in her direction, and Sophia took her fill of him. Handsome, strong, and well proportioned. He was everything she had imagined him to be, but it was the vulnerability in his dark eyes that caught at her, a tug to her heart and an ache in her belly.

"Come here," she held out her hand and he came to her at once, his fingers tangling with hers, climbing up onto the bed beside her. Their mouths closed on each other, deep kisses, tongues tangling, and the weight of him over her body was perfect. She opened her legs, clasping her ankles at his back, feeling the hard length of him pressing for entry.

He nuzzled at her throat, then lifted himself so that he could claim one breast and then the other, sucking hard on that sensitive tip. Sophia moaned, hands sliding over his broad shoulders and back, feeling the muscles bunch as he moved.

"I need you," he gasped out.

Startled, she opened her eyes, which she realized had been closed until now, and found his face very close. "Then have me," she said.

With a groan he sought entry, and then he was pressing inside her, lifting her bottom for a better angle, and it was familiar and yet very different. *His* eyes were closed now, as he moved gently at first and then more vigorously as the pleasure soared between them. For a moment it was as if she was two women, one enjoying herself a great deal, and the other watching him anxiously, cautiously from a distance.

Was he like Oldney?

But not once did he scrutinize her in that cold, mechanical way. Ticking off each part of their love making on his mental to-do list. Nicholas was as deeply engrossed in their act as she, and finally Sophia was able to set aside her fears and allow herself to be swept away.

As her climax claimed her, she felt him reach his, and then they lay gasping, like desperate swimmers who had reached the shore. He did not speak for a time, contenting himself with little kisses to her face and neck, breathing in the scent of her hair as if he wanted to remember it forever.

It was so different from what she had been used to with Oldney. Instead of being a puppet to be manipulated, she felt as if she wasn't alone. She was part of a couple, and together they were whole.

Sophia had the urge to talk, to ask him what he was feeling, delve into his thoughts, but she was so tired. Besides, she wasn't sure he would appreciate being interrogated just now. Her eyes closed and, content, she fell asleep in his arms.

But when she awoke, Nicholas was gone, and the doubts came creeping back.

Chapter Twelve

MARIANNE JUMPED UP as Sophia entered the breakfast room. She had not seen the other woman since she had arrived, being busy with her own concerns, and with the late nights she had been keeping, she found herself sleeping well into the day. But this morning she had awoken early, and when she came downstairs Marianne was there. There was also a young boy sitting beside her, and seeing him made Sophia's steps come to a sudden halt.

"Your Grace!" Marianne cried, her brown eyes wide with shock. "I did not think you would be down this early."

She was already on her way to the door, her arm around the boy at her side. He was complaining about not having finished eating, but Marianne hushed him desperately. It was as if she was trying to be invisible, or cause the least trouble possible, lest Sophia take offense at their presence and tell them to leave immediately.

Sophia put up a hand to stop her. "Not on my account, please! You are my guest, so please finish your breakfasts."

Marianne looked in two minds whether to obey. Then the boy murmured something about "hungry" and the two of them returned to their seats and sat down. Marianne gave her son a reassuring smile as he fell upon his boiled egg and toast.

Sophia also sat and poured herself tea from the pot. She took a sip as she contemplated the other two. Marianne had some color in her cheeks, different from the wan ghost who had confronted her that evening on the front steps. She must have been very pretty when a young girl, but the past year at least had done her no favors. The boy—he was eight, Sophia recalled—was pleasant looking, with hair more fair than brown and, when he looked up shyly at her, eyes of more brown than green. Oldney's had been the latter, she recalled—calculating and as cold as green marbles.

For a moment she compared them to Nicholas Blake's eyes, so dark and warm, and full of emotion as they gazed into hers.

"Your Grace?"

Marianne was watching her uneasily, and Sophia set down her teacup with a clatter. "What was that? I was woolgathering."

"I asked you when you wish us to leave. I will need to make arrangements. I thought perhaps I could go home, but—" Tears filled her eyes, and she blinked them hastily away.

"Home?" Sophia repeated. "Why can't you go home, Marianne?"

"I-I don't know if my—my family will want me back. I did not leave under the best of circumstances."

Like so many young ladies, Sophia thought with an inner sigh. Marianne had probably believed Oldney's lies that he would love her forever and set her up in a grand house and pay all her bills. Which he had, she supposed, but with his death, Marianne's precarious position had become even more precarious.

"I do not want you to think of that," she said briskly. "You and your son are welcome here for as long as you wish to stay. Oldney did not make provision for you, and it is up to me to see you are not thrown out on the street. Speaking of which," she chose a slice of toast and began to butter it, "where have you been for the past year?"

Marianne swallowed, her eyes wide and still bright with tears. "I . . . we stayed in the house in Curzon Street for some months after he . . ." A glance at her son. "I did not know what was going to happen, but every day that passed seemed like a gift. Then a gentleman came and informed me we had to leave. He threatened to call the bailiffs and have us evicted. It seemed better to go before he could do so. I was lucky that I had a friend in Lambeth. For a time, she worked in the Curzon Street house, and we became close. She left to marry a housepainter, and now she has two children, but she told me if I ever needed help to come to her."

"It is good to have such friends," Sophia said quietly. "You were fortunate."

Marianne swallowed. "Yes, very fortunate, because without her . . ." She shook her head at the images that must be crowding her mind. "Her house is small, and cramped with us all in it, and although she has been so kind, I knew we could not stay there forever. That is why I came to you. I never expected you to ask me to stay. I thought you might pay me to go away, and I was prepared for that, because I was desperate."

She wiped the tears from her cheeks, but they did not stop. Hugo, who by now had realized how upset his mother was, wriggled closer and wrapped his arms about her.

Sophia felt an uncharacteristic urge to comfort Marianne but quashed it. Such behavior would only make them both uncomfortable, and it was better not to draw attention to the high emotion. Instead, she turned to more practical matters.

"Tell me, does Hugo attend school?"

Marianne cleared her throat and mopped at her face with her table napkin. After a moment she pulled herself together. "Yes," she cleared her throat. "He attended the parish school for a time, but recently I have been teaching him at home."

"*You* have been teaching him?" Sophia couldn't keep the surprise out of her voice. Women were not generally educated, being taught housekeeping skills instead.

"Yes. He is young enough now, but later he will need someone with a better grasp of subjects such as math and science."

Sophia was impressed. A thought came into her head, and she waited a moment to allow it to percolate. "I wonder . . . My housekeeper has recently left and Webster, my butler, is run ragged. I wonder if you would consider taking on the role. If you do not wish it, then that is fine, you can still stay, but it might give you something to do during the day."

"Hugo needs me to—"

Sophia waved an impatient hand. "Yes, yes, but in return for you taking on the position of housekeeper for me, I would be happy to pay for Hugo to go to a good school. A school of your choosing, Marianne."

The woman stared back at her. Her mouth was slightly ajar.

"There is no hurry," Sophia said quickly, worried Marianne was about to burst into tears again, or perhaps even rush to give her a hug. She always found hugs awkward. "You can take your time to think about my offer. I do not expect you to—"

But Marianne shook her head rather wildly. "I don't need to think. Yes! Thank you. I would be more than happy to be your housekeeper, Your Grace."

Sophia smiled, but before she could speak, Marianne took a shuddering breath and hurried on, leaning forward with her hands clasped on the table.

"But won't the gossips make matters difficult for you? You will be taking your husband's mistress on as your housekeeper. They will think it bad enough that you have invited me into your home, but to employ me as your housekeeper . . . I think there will be a great deal of unpleasant talk."

Sophia bit into her toast, chewed, and swallowed. "Frankly, I couldn't care less what the gossips say," she said. "I *used* to care a great deal, but over the past year I have come to understand how little that matters. My husband was . . ." she glanced at Hugo, "not a nice man. Perhaps he was nicer to you but—"

"He was not an easy man," Marianne hurriedly admitted, also glancing at her son. "But he was a good father. He took an interest in Hugo. I think, even if he had grown tired of me, that relationship with his son would have continued."

Sophia felt a wave of sadness wash over her. It took her by surprise. She had not had children with her husband, and she had been relieved by their absence. What would have happened to them, after all? Left alone most of the time while their parents were out socializing? Oldney had said he wanted an heir, and he had blamed her, but he had not seemed to care too much. Now she knew why. He already had a son tucked away in Curzon Street.

Marianne must have seen something in her face, because she hurried into speech, as if afraid of what Sophia might say next. She was evidently still worried about being thrown out onto the street.

"I am most grateful for your kindness, your—your generosity, Your Grace. I will do my utmost to fill the role you ask of me, and I will seek out a school for Hugo. I do not have enough words to tell you how very appreciative I am of your—"

Sophia waved a hand. "Enough," she said wearily. "I am glad we have come to a mutually convenient agreement. You have saved me from having to advertise for the position and then interview a great many unsuitable applicants. It would be very tiresome."

Marianne was smiling at her, well aware that Sophia's protests were meant to soothe, but quickly bowed her head to hide her amusement.

Just then Sophia caught sight of Webster lurking in the doorway, his eyes out on stalks. He had probably heard some of their conversation and was wondering whether his mistress had lost her mind. Sophia had wondered about that, too, but actually being a do-gooder—within reason—was very freeing. She might even join one of those charities that she had heard other ladies waffle on about, but for now Marianne and Hugo were enough.

"Yes, Webster, what is it?"

"The mail has come." Cautiously he approached, and she saw that he was holding a silver tray. "There are a number of invitations, Your Grace, although none of consequence."

He sniffed and Sophia couldn't help but smile. Webster was a far greater snob than anyone she knew in the *ton*. His uneasy glance at Marianne seemed to confirm her fears he had overheard their conversation. Did he think she was going to grab the silver and run off with it?

The thought amused her, but she pushed it aside. Sophia did not believe Marianne was going to do anything of the kind. She considered herself a good judge of character and she did not often get it wrong, although in Nicholas Blake's case perhaps she had let her animosity blind her to his good points for too long.

The mail was uninteresting, and she tossed most of it aside. Apart from a letter in a familiar hand. She smiled as she broke the seal. Her sister Ellis was writing to her from her home in Wales, and she had some exciting news. She was with child. As Sophia read on, Ellis wasn't just wanting to share her good news, she was asking if Sophia would come and stay with her at the expected time of the birth.

"Please come. I will need your encouragement and support," Ellis had written.

There was a time when Ellis would not have wanted her sister anywhere near her, especially at such a challenging time. Matters had changed when Ellis had come to London and needed Sophia's protection, which Sophia had been more than happy to give. Ellis had needed Nicholas's help, too, which at the time had made Sophia particularly angry. But it had all turned out well. Ellis had married her artist lord, Owen, and lived happily with him in Wales. And now they were about to bring the fruit of their union into the world.

Catherine, Sophia's elder sister, had two children. Her youngest was a daughter, the child of her husband Viscount Albury, while the eldest, a son Jack, was the son of her first husband, the Duke of Wellesley. Catherine and her family lived with Albury at his home in the north of England and seemed more than happy to remain there. She rarely visited London these days and so Sophia rarely saw her.

Again, Sophia pondered on the fact she did not have any children of her own, and whether she wanted them. She had never considered herself the sort of woman who would be a good mother. Her own mother had loved her and her sisters, in her way, but when Sophia's father was killed tragically, she had seemed to put all her energies into finding her three daughters husbands who were rich dukes.

Sophia did not think she would do that. She knew now the difference between a good marriage and a bad one, and she would never force any child she might have into a marriage that caused them pain, no matter how wealthy their partner was. Better to marry a commoner than someone like Oldney.

As I am often reminded by my enemies, I am a commoner aping my betters.

She glanced at Hugo, who was busily dunking toast soldiers into his boiled egg. He looked like any normal little boy. He caught her eye and smiled, and it was a sweet smile. Sophia asked herself if it was still possible for her to have a child of her own. Not with Oldney, of course, but with someone else. Her thoughts drifted to Diablo's last night, where drunken men handed over their blunt in games of chance, and women hung over their shoulders and cheered them on. Nicholas Blake frequented such places for his work and his search for the sister who was probably long dead. Sophia could not see him ever stopping. What sort of a parent would that make him?

She startled. Was she really thinking of him as the father to a possible child?

There was passion between them. A burning, hot desire that seemed in no danger of cooling. Although last night had been different—the passion was still there but it had been more tender, as if they wanted it to last. Oh yes, she wanted to see him again but at the same time she was afraid of what would happen if she did. What if she wanted more than he was willing to offer her?

"You are deep in thought," Marianne said.

Sophia had been so lost in her own thoughts she had forgotten the other woman was there. She forced herself to calmly take a sip of her cooling tea before she spoke. "I received a letter from my sister. She is having a baby, and she wants me to stay with her in Wales."

"Oh?"

"That will not affect you, Marianne," she assured her.

Marianne's tense shoulders relaxed. "I will ensure everything runs smoothly in your absence, Your Grace."

Sophia smiled. "I'm sure you will."

Webster was back in the doorway, and she was sure she heard him sniff from her seat at the breakfast table. The man really was insufferable, but she supposed she could expect nothing less. And she'd best get used to it. Soon everyone would be talking about the Dowager Duchess of Oldney and her new housekeeper. The *ton* was a hive of gossip.

Chapter Thirteen

NICHOLAS STARED AT the woman walking ahead of him. Fern would be about twenty-seven years old now, and more or less the same height and shape as the figure he was following. But this had happened to him before, and when the woman he'd thought was his sister turned around, he'd realized he'd been deceived by a vague likeness and probably a great deal of hope. It was always the same.

And yet he could not stop hoping.

She was walking briskly, and he followed at a distance. They were in a less than salubrious area, but she seemed to know where she was going. After a few more yards she turned into a laneway. Nicholas followed and hesitated at the mouth of the narrow entrance. The woman had gone.

He ventured in farther and looked about the grimy courtyard. There were doorways leading into houses—she must have taken one of them. Hesitating, he wondered if he should knock on some of the doors, but what would he say? They would slam their doors in his face. And he already knew in his heart that it wasn't his sister he had seen.

Hope began to drain out of him.

Sophia would be at Hettie Devenish's again tonight and he shouldn't be wandering around the streets when he needed to be alert to keep her safe. After she had told him Chatham's plans, he had tried to imagine how they were going to ruin Gordon, but it could be anything. He'd need to know more so that he could put a strategy in place to foil them and save his friend. For now, he was relying on Sophia to get him the information, and it felt strange to trust someone else to do his job for him.

He wasn't sure of the last time he had trusted anyone to that extent.

The night in her bed, in her arms, had been another first for him. It had been so different from their previous encounters, when all they had wanted to do was scratch the raging itch, when it had simply seemed imperative to be inside her. But this time he had wanted to stretch out the moment, take his time with her, and afterward he had held her against him and enjoyed the intimacy of her naked body pressed to his.

He had lain there long after she fell asleep, watching her. The flutter of her eyelids, and the way her hair spread out on the pillow. He was embarrassed now to remember how he had pressed his nose to the angle between her neck and shoulder, drawing the scent of her skin deep into his lungs.

As if he had wanted to remember it forever.

He hardly recognized himself in the man he had become when he was with her, and yet he had never been happier. If he let himself, Nicholas could see their life stretching out before him, images of Sophia smiling at him over meals, kissing him as they lay in their bed together, looking at him with love in her dark eyes. It was ridiculous. And dangerous. He must not allow himself to believe in something that would never happen. He needed a cool head and a pragmatic outlook.

Yes, he was enjoying the affection he had found with the duchess, but there was nothing more to it than that. This time would end, and he would return to his solitary life and his search for his sister. He didn't need a broken heart as a memento.

Nicholas heard a voice and looked up at the window above him. The woman he had followed was standing there glaring at him, and it wasn't Fern. She opened the casement and leaned out, and he realized she was about to empty her chamber pot over his head.

With a muffled curse he took to his heels.

HETTIE DEVENISH'S ROOMS were a crush. It was late, but the gentlemen in London didn't start their evenings until after the more formal, and tame, engagements were over and done with. Balls and the like had to be attended, ladies had to be squired about, but once they were tucked up in bed, that was when the fun began. That was when the gentlemen strutted out to find a game of chance, or a drink, or a woman with whom to pass the time.

Sophia watched Chatham, Butler, Arnold, and Gordon play a game of vingt-un. Gordon frowned at his hand and then made a weak joke, which had the others laughing uproariously, as if he was the most amusing man in the world. Although Sophia smiled, too, she was getting more worried by the minute.

Once again Gordon lost heavily, but he just shrugged and smiled, as if it was of no consequence to him. Probably it was not. Nicholas had told her that Gordon's father had died and left his son one of the richest men in England. But what of his mother? Sophia wondered where she was at this moment. Didn't she care that her son was wasting his family's fortune among some very dubious company? Perhaps the lady didn't know. She considered whether she should tell her—an anonymous note? And then what, would it simply prompt the three rakes before her to act all the sooner?

Chatham called for more claret—his drink of choice—and when the waiter was slow, went to get it himself. Butcher and Arnold had gone to relieve themselves, and for the first time Sophia and Gordon were alone.

He was staring down at his cards, but she saw him flick a glance up at her from beneath his lashes, as if he was aware of her scrutiny. She hesitated, but this was the perfect time to speak, despite knowing how careful she must be.

"You are enjoying the game, Sir Gordon?" she asked quietly. "I do not see you winning very often. I'm not sure I would be brave enough to play another round if I were always losing."

Her words were probably blunter than they needed to be, but Gordon gave her a sweet smile. "I do not mind. I am having more fun than I expected to have when I first arrived in London."

"Life in the city can be heady indeed," she said. "Until one learns to moderate one's imbibing."

He blinked at her, as if he was trying to understand her meaning, and yet there was something in his eyes that gave her pause. "Ha!" he laughed. "And yet you have been joining your friends quite often, Duchess. You must be enjoying their company, too."

There *was* something in his pale eyes, a question but also a glint of intelligence. Was he . . . Could he be playing a part, just as she was?

"I believe you are also friends with Mr. Blake," she said tartly.

His smile froze and he looked down at the table. "I was friends with him a long time ago. I have cast aside that friendship."

"Oh? I do not blame you. The man is rather a lot, and he seems determined to spoil our fun. Well, to his own detriment be it."

Gordon was looking at her now and his eyes had narrowed. She had noticed again how little he had been drinking tonight, and now she was more certain than ever that his inebriated behavior was nothing more than an act.

"You have spoken with him?" His voice was uncharacteristically sharp. "Chatham said he came upon the two of you alone at Diablo's. If you speak to him again, then tell him it would be better if he minded his own business."

"Unless he is not as quick to cast aside his friendship with you, as you were with him."

That struck home. She saw him flinch. He gave a quick look around, to ensure they were still alone, and then leaned forward. His voice dropped. "Nicholas would understand why I am here. If you see him again tell him he must not interfere."

Sophia leaned closer too, aware of his serious and sober expression. "Can't you tell him yourself?"

Gordon had opened his mouth to reply, and then his eyes darted beyond her, and his face creased once again into a lopsided smile. "Arnold," he said loudly, "the duchess was telling me about a ball she once attended with Oldney. I did not realize you could use your host's bedchamber as if it was your own."

Arnold snorted a laugh, glancing at Sophia as he seated himself.

"Where are the others?" Sophia asked, with a casual glance about the room. "Are they too tired to continue?"

Arnold's laugh was less amused this time. "They are talking with Hettie. From the expressions on their faces it looks serious." He gave a mock grimace. "Maybe they have been misbehaving."

She wondered if Hettie was warning them about Gordon and hoped she was not. There was something going on here she did not yet understand, and her meddling would not help, no matter how well meant.

"How is your stomach?" Gordon asked, picking up his cards.

He was focused on his hand and did not notice Arnold's startled look. "My stomach is perfectly fine, thank you, Robinson. Why do you ask?"

"Oh," Gordon blinked at him, "I thought you said you were troubled by it. You said you were a sickly child. Didn't you? Have I got it wrong again?" He giggled.

Just for an instant, Arnold stared at him with pure dislike, before he remembered himself and gave a what-can-you-do shrug. "I said my *brother* was a sickly child. Although what that has got to do with anything escapes me."

Gordon shrugged back and nearly fell off his chair. "I could have misheard. Probably in my cups again." He waved clumsily at his full glass and knocked it over.

The next few moments were taken up with rescuing what could be recovered and keeping out of the way of the spreading puddle of red wine. The topic of conversation was forgotten, but Sophia couldn't help but wonder if that had been Gordon's aim. And what on earth did he mean about Arnold's stomach? She was bewildered now as well as worried. Was the situation just as it seemed? It was quite possible that Gordon was simply a fool who was being fleeced by older, more experienced men.

And yet she felt there was something more. She needed to speak with Nicholas, and if she were to guess he would be around here somewhere, keeping a watchful eye. She was surprised to realize she didn't mind. In fact, there was a level of comfort in knowing he would come to her rescue if she needed it. Not, she told herself quickly, that she did.

When Chatham and Butcher returned, looking put out, they informed her that they were leaving. "Hettie is being cork-brained," Butcher said, mouth pursed. He glanced at Gordon and then at Sophia. "We thought we might go to Diablo's again. At least no one there offers unsought advice."

Sophia yawned. "Not me. I am going home to bed."

Arnold smirked and seemed about to make an off-color re-mark but caught Chatham's eye and changed his mind. "Robinson?" he queried. "You'll come, won't you?"

Gordon's head was nodding, as if he was about to fall asleep.

Sophia saw her chance. "He can hardly walk," she said quickly. "I will see he gets home. Unless you want to do it?" She looked from Chatham to the others. "He is *your* friend, after all."

The marquess grimaced. Just as she had suspected, he had no interest in a drunken Gordon. "I will leave him in your tender care," he said.

They heaved the younger man up from the table, and across the room. No one seemed to notice or care—they were all too busy with their own concerns. When they reached the doorway,

Hettie was there, watching with a frown, but she did not interfere as the gentlemen headed off to Diablo's.

"I've ensured his wine is well watered down," Hettie said, for Sophia's ears alone. "I'm not sure you can get drunk. He must have a very low tolerance."

"I'll see he gets home safely. Can you send for my coach, Hettie?"

Hettie did as she asked, and the coach arrived quickly.

By this time they were standing, swaying on the street, while Hettie's footmen kept an eye on anyone who might take advantage. One of them opened the door, and she was just about to ask for his help in getting Gordon inside, when a strong pair of arms reached out and dragged the young man up the step and onto the padded seat.

Sophia opened her mouth to scream.

Chapter Fourteen

T HE DUCHESS DID not scream, to Nicholas's relief, otherwise he would have had to put a hand over her mouth. Being quick witted, she saw at once who was in her coach, and told the servant it was perfectly all right. The bruiser gave Nicholas a dubious look, but a moment later the door was closed on them, and the vehicle began to move.

"What on earth are you doing?" Sophia said, her low voice doing nothing to disguise her anger. "You'll ruin everything!"

He wanted to smile. "I think you'll find I am better at dragging information out of people than you, Duchess."

She huffed, the emotion draining out of her. "I was going to take him to Berkeley Square and sober him up." Her dark eyes clouded with worry. "Nicholas, there is something very odd going on."

Nicholas went to answer, just as their unconscious friend raised his head and spoke in a calm and completely sober voice. "I knew it."

Sophia turned to look at him, but she didn't seem as amazed as Nicholas by the transformation. "Just what are you playing at, Sir Gordon?"

Gordon straightened his cuffs. "I could ask you the same question," he said levelly. His gaze slid to Nicholas. "I knew you couldn't keep away. And the duchess is quite right. You'll ruin everything, Nicholas."

Nicholas paused. Whatever he had expected Gordon to say, it wasn't this. "I was worried about you," he replied, but it sounded feeble.

"You shouldn't have been. I know what I am doing. I just hope you haven't messed it up before I can get the answers I need. That *you* need."

Nicholas was still at a loss. "What in God's name are you talking about? Perhaps all that drinking really has rotted your brain, Gordon."

Gordon snorted. "I barely touch the stuff. If you really knew me you'd know I don't drink. Not after my grandfather drank himself into the grave. I swore off it then, and I haven't changed my mind since."

Nicholas sighed and slumped back into his seat. Outside the London streets passed them by, and someone called out while someone else shouted with laughter, but inside the coach it was very quiet.

"Tell me then," Nicholas spoke at last, "because I haven't the faintest idea what you are on about."

Gordon smirked, as if he had won the argument. "It isn't often one can say they have bamboozled Nicholas Blake," he said. Then his face turned serious. "As I was saying to the Dowager Duchess earlier, Sir Tomas Arnold has a sickly brother. I knew him, and at school he was always in the infirmary." He looked at Sophia. "I was trying to pass that piece of information on to you without giving myself away."

Bewildered, Sophia shook her head. "Why is that information even important?"

Gordon sighed, then turned to Nicholas. "Arnold's brother's name was Joseph," he said sharply. "Surely you remember him?"

"Joseph." Nicholas's eyes narrowed. "In the infirmary, you say? At school? At *our* school?"

"Yes."

Nicholas felt his heartbeat speed up. "Tell me what you know, Gordon, and stop playing games."

Gordon ran a hand over his face. "It's a long story. Wouldn't it be better if I waited until we found somewhere more comfortable? We can go to my rooms if the duchess prefers not to—"

"I very much want to hear what you have to say," Sophia cut in. "I want to know why I have wasted so many hours of my life doing something I loathe, with gentlemen I loathe, and it seems it was all for nothing."

Nicholas reached out and took her hand. "Not for nothing," he assured her gently.

Her rigid poise relaxed a little. "We will go to Berkeley Square, and then we will talk," she informed them, before leaning back and closing her eyes.

Nicholas looked across at Gordon, who seemed startled by the level of intimacy between them, and grinned. "The duchess has spoken," he said. "We will wait until we are all comfortable and then, my young friend, you will explain to me why you have me worried out of my wits."

Gordon seemed a little shamefaced, but he nodded and said no more.

SOPHIA HURRIED INTO the Yellow Room and was glad to see that the fire was already burning. She tugged off her cloak and gloves and tossed them aside. Webster had followed her in, appearing baffled by two unexpected guests at such a late hour, but bowed in response to her request for refreshments, before he hurried out again.

Gordon began to speak, but she held up her hand. "Coffee first, and some of Cook's delicious fruit cake, and then you can explain yourself, Sir Gordon."

Nicholas chuckled and sank down on the armchair, as if he

were perfectly at home. She almost laughed at the sight but firmed her lips and prepared to wait. Gordon sat down on a chaise longue which was, as Sophia knew only too well, extremely uncomfortable. Serve him right, he deserved to have numb buttocks for the trick he'd played them.

When the coffee arrived, and the fruit cake, she made certain everyone had some of each, and there was silence apart from sipping and chewing. Then at last, when she felt ready to hear whatever there was to hear, she nodded regally to Gordon.

For the last twenty minutes he had looked ready to burst with all the information he was holding inside. Now, he took a deep breath and turned to Nicholas. "It is about your sister."

Nicholas sat forward, startled out of his relaxed pose. "Fern?"

"I discovered something. Only a snippet, but I knew if I came to you with it, you would try to find out the whole story for yourself, and they would never tell you—these men hate you. So it had to be me. I thought about it, and I came up with a way to uncover the truth. I would infiltrate their group, ingratiate myself into their clique, and at the same time make myself harmless, so that they would talk of confidential matters in front of me. *That* is what I have been doing these past few months since I came to London."

He looked so pleased with himself, Sophia couldn't help but bring him down a peg. "Apart from losing lots of your money." But her heart wasn't in it, and neither Gordon nor Nicholas seemed to hear her comment.

"Tell me," Nicholas said again, and even in the flickering light of the fire he looked pale. "Don't leave anything out."

Gordon settled himself to do just that. "I had not seen Joseph Arnold for years, not since school, but I happened to be attending a horse race in the country and recognized him. He was pleased to see a familiar face and we began to chat about the old days, and then he mentioned his brother, Tomas."

Sir Tomas Arnold. Sophia felt herself go cold. She had never liked Tomas. The way in which he stared at her . . . She had never trusted him but had always had a hard time pinning down exactly why. Was her mistrust about to be justified?

"Joseph told me that Tomas had visited him at school when he was ill in the infirmary and saw a girl there. Tomas had been smitten. He persuaded Joseph to be go-between, and Tomas and the girl would meet in the infirmary, where Joseph spent much of his time with his sickly stomach."

"Who was this girl?" Sophia asked.

Nicholas's gaze barely left Gordon's face as he explained, his voice dull with shock. "The girl was my sister, Fern. She used to sit with the students who were poorly and read to them or play games."

"Was she happy to have Tomas drooling over her?" Sophia spoke sarcastically, but she was beginning to feel a little queasy herself. She could already tell where this story was going.

Gordon shrugged. "According to Joseph, she thought herself in love, and why would he lie? He even seemed proud of the fact that he had helped in the affair, although when I asked him where Fern was now, he said he didn't know, and changed the subject. I suspect he feels some guilt over the matter—after all, he sent an innocent young girl into the arms of a heartless rake." His face twisted. "He said she was meeting Tomas the evening she left, and she was planning to go to London to be with him. Evidently by then Tomas had convinced her he loved her as well as making her all sorts of promises. According to Joseph, those promises included a house and a carriage, as well as pretty clothes and jewels. A sort of fairytale ending."

Nicholas swallowed. He looked sick, and Sophia wanted to go to him and wrap her arms around him. "Young girls dream of such things," she explained. "It is a normal part of growing up. I did so myself." *For about two minutes, before Oldney brought me back to reality,* she thought, but she did not say it aloud.

Nicholas seemed stunned. "She should have told me, or our father. Why keep it a secret? Why didn't she tell me?"

"Because you would have stopped her," Sophia replied gently, "and she had made up her mind to embark on this adventure."

He struggled a moment, as if he wanted to argue, but she could see he knew it was the truth. "And then?" He turned back to Gordon. "What became of Fern after she came to London?"

Gordon's expression was apologetic. "I don't know. Only Tomas Arnold knows what happened to her. That is why I have been wheedling my way into Tomas's group of friends."

Nicholas lurched to his feet, his hands in fists at his sides. "You should have told me! You should have—"

Gordon cut him short with a sharp, "And then what? They would never tell you. They would find enjoyment in taunting you, hurting you. You are my *friend*, Nicholas! I want to do this for *you*. I will never forget how kind you were to me at school. You saved me from the bullies, and you brought me books to read. You made sure I was as happy as I could be. I just wanted to give you something in return."

Nicholas looked as if he didn't know what to say. Sophia's own eyes stung with emotion because it was perfectly clear that Gordon meant every word.

"Gordon . . ." He sighed and rubbed his chest as if there was an ache there. "Fern went off with Tomas," he said, as if trying to convince himself. "All these years I have wondered why she was waiting at the school gate that evening. And now I know. I thank you, Gordon, I truly do. And yet somehow . . . the truth seems almost worse than not knowing."

"That's just foolish," Sophia informed him brusquely. "It is always better to know."

He managed a smile. "My clear-headed duchess," he said. "Ever the practical voice of reason."

Sophia wondered if that were really true. She hadn't been very practical when it came to him.

"I need to question Tomas," Gordon said eagerly. "I know you want to do it, but he won't tell you anything, Nicholas. It needs to be me."

"I can beat it out of him," Nicholas retorted, but he sounded dispirited.

"And be arrested and thrown in jail?"

Sophia interrupted before they could get into an argument. "Gordon is right. He needs to do this. Although," she said, "you do know our friends have a plan when it comes to you, Gordon? I heard it from Chatham. They are going to place you in a precarious position, one in which you will be ruined unless you ask for Nicholas's help. And if Nicholas helps you *he* will be ruined, too."

Gordon frowned. "They are using me to get at him?"

"Yes, it is Nicholas they really want to hurt. You are just the means to the end."

"And I will have to decide whether to help you and destroy my own reputation—such as it is—or let you sink." Nicholas watched his friend take this in.

"I'm not surprised," Gordon said at last. "Let them! Once the truth comes out about Fern and Tomas, we will have the advantage. They'll have to stop whatever this plan of theirs is if they don't want everyone to know what they're capable of."

Nicholas sat down with a groan. "Not such a good idea, Gordon. You might be hurt. You might be killed. You know I cannot allow that to happen."

But Gordon wasn't to be dissuaded. "Just give me just another day or two," he wheedled. "I'm close, I know it. They think I am such a fool and a sot that I don't know what they're saying. I know I can get them to give away what happened to Fern. Please, Nicholas."

Nicholas turned to Sophia and raised his brows.

"It seems a reasonable request," she answered his unspoken question. "And I will be there to keep an eye on him." She fixed Gordon with an imperious look. "Just don't go anywhere with them unless I come, too."

Nicholas added, "And come to me as soon as you feel you are in danger. Or if you discover what happened to Fern. Don't delay even for a minute, do you hear me? These are men who have no conscience. They are rats, and if they feel trapped or threatened, they won't hesitate to attack."

Gordon nodded, trying to look chastened, but there was a spark of excitement in his eyes.

Seeing they had come to an agreement, Sophia rang the bell for a servant. "Are you staying or going back to your rooms?" she asked Gordon.

Gordon looked at Nicholas, hesitated, and then rose to his feet. "I am going back to my rooms," he said. "Thank you, Your Grace. I appreciate you watching out for me. And you too, Nicholas." He sent his friend a warm smile. "No, don't come with me," he added, his smile turning into a grin as he headed for the door. "I'm too old now for you to tuck me in."

Nicholas snorted a laugh but remained in his seat. Sophia walked over to him, looking down into his upturned face. "Not going with him?" she asked quietly.

Nicholas's mouth curved up at the corners. "I think I will stay."

Sophia told herself she was every kind of fool as she smiled back.

Chapter Fifteen

NICHOLAS STRETCHED HIS arms above his head, enjoying the sated feeling in his body, and let his gaze rest on the woman at his side. Their lovemaking had exceeded even previous expectations, and not because it had been fast and glorious. Once more they had taken their time. He had kissed her until his head spun and touched her body as if he needed to memorize every inch of it. Not that he was likely to forget.

It felt as if she had slipped into his heart and soul and become a part of him.

He had realized, last night, when Gordon was there, that the three of them worked well together. He was no longer alone in this endeavor to find his sister, find Fern. He felt closer to an answer than ever before, and that awful sense of isolation had gone. Whatever they discovered, be it good or bad, he would not have to face it by himself.

Sunshine was leaking in through the curtains, dust motes dancing in the light, which meant it was probably late. He should have left hours ago and returned to his rooms. Mrs. Shirley would be wondering where he was and clicking her tongue that his breakfast was going to waste. But he didn't care. He felt no urgency to rise and rush about. He wanted to stay right here, with Sophia, and wallow in the moment.

A tap on the bedchamber door startled him out of his complacency. Sophia woke and sat up, her hair cascading untidily about her, her dark eyes sleepy. She turned to look at Nicholas as if she were surprised to see him there, and then she smiled and leaned in to whisper in his ear.

"Stay here and be quiet."

She laughed quietly as she pulled the covers up over his head. He gave a muffled chuckle in response, but lay still as she rose, her robe rustling as she drew it on, and went to the door. He could hear a female voice, and Sophia's response, and then the door closed again. The mattress moved as she dispensed of her robe and climbed back onto the bed and drew down the covers.

He blinked up at her. "Who was it?"

"My new housekeeper, Marianne. She wants to begin work today. I would not want to dissuade her when she's so keen." She pulled a face as if she had something nasty in her mouth. "I haven't told you about Marianne, have I?"

"No. Don't you like her?"

"I like her very much, but it is a wonder you have not heard the gossip. I'm sure it won't be long before tongues are wagging." She settled herself against his chest, curling strands of his mat of dark hair with her fingers, and avoiding his gaze. "Marianne was Oldney's mistress, and she bore him a son called Hugo. Now he is dead they have nowhere to go."

He didn't know what to say. He opened his mouth and then closed it as she continued to speak.

"I am doing this because I feel it is right." She sounded as if she half expected him to reprimand her. Or warn her of the consequences of her action. "Marianne has done nothing wrong—none of this is her fault. She was living in Curzon Street." She flicked Nicholas a glance. "Very handy for Oldney to pay her a visit whenever he felt like it. But after he died, Thatcher, his man of business, tossed her out onto the street. She has been staying with a friend in Lambeth. Hugo, Oldney's son, is only eight and I just . . . I have no children of my own, so why shouldn't I help? I have the means, and this is such a big house. It seems the perfect solution for them and me."

He chose his words carefully. "You will be gaining a house-keeper who works harder than any other. Not because she aspires to a clean house but because of your kindness to her."

She laughed but the humor soon faded from her eyes as she gazed into his. "It's not that. You know it isn't. I want to help. It is a good feeling, and it costs me very little."

"Sophia the patron of the desperate," he intoned seriously.

She pulled his chest hair and made him cry out, before he caught her hand in his. Warmth flared inside him, and he reached up as she met him halfway, kissing her lips with increasing passion.

His heart filled with something he didn't want to admit—it was far too worrying that he should feel like this. Nicholas cupped her face, either side of the waterfall of her dark hair, and deepened the kiss. Desire was never far away from him when he was with Sophia, and now his cock hardened with wanting to be inside her. She wriggled under the covers, her naked body sliding against his, and sat up to straddle him.

Nicholas groaned. Her hand was on his hard length, stroking, and then she lifted herself up and set him at her entrance. Slowly, oh so slowly, she eased herself down until he was fully inside her.

"Sophia," he gasped. "God, so good. Why is it always so good with you?"

She was sitting up straighter now, and her breasts were right there. He had to touch, and he leaned up to cover the tips with his mouth, one at a time, making her arch toward him, her eyes fluttering closed.

"I don't know, but this feels wonderful," she breathed.

She rested her hands on his chest, and he caught hold of her hips, helping as she lifted and lowered herself upon his shaft. She was panting a little, a pinch between her brows, as if she was concentrating on getting this exquisite moment just right.

He loved her.

Sophia cried out, clenching around him, and he came, too, with a wordless cry. Pleasure took hold of them, and they tumbled together into whatever heaven had been created just for them.

When she was again tucked against his side, her breath soft and warm against his cheek, he felt the need to say things. Things he had never said to anyone before. Personal, heartfelt things. But he bit his lip on them. Would they be welcome? This was very new, and not so long ago they had hated each other. No, Sophia would not want to hear them because this was supposed to be nothing more than a brief affair. She might even move on all the quicker if she believed he wanted more from her. That he might have fallen in *love* with her.

Sophia's voice was soft against his skin. "My new housekeeper is seeing that a late breakfast is prepared. Will you stay?"

He let himself imagine it. Him sitting opposite Sophia, eating and sharing smiles, eyes meeting with memories of their intimate moments. He admitted he wanted nothing more than to stay for breakfast, but at the same time the sensible part of him instructed him that he must not. At least, not until he was sure of her feelings and what this mysterious phenomenon was between them.

"I need to go," he said levelly. "But we should discuss what to do next about Gordon. And Fern."

She was sitting up now, watching him, but he avoided her keen gaze.

"Yes, we should," she answered mildly. "I am to meet Chatham and the others again tonight. They sent me an invitation to a hell I haven't been to before. Lucifer's." She wrinkled her nose.

He didn't like the name of the hell, nor the thought of her meeting with those vicious gentlemen. "When did they send this?"

"Last night. Webster gave me the note. Should I not go?" she asked with a teasing arch of her eyebrow. "Perhaps tonight I will learn what they intend to do to ruin Gordon. Not forgetting what they are going to do to you."

That was true. She was in too deep now to back out, but he wished she would. The whole thing worried him, and if it weren't for Gordon, and Fern, he might have told her to do just that. He was still angry about Fern going off with Arnold, angry with both the gentleman and his sister. Why hadn't she told him or his father? Sophia was probably right—Fern had been weary of her life at the school and wanted adventure. Love and adventure. And there was no point in wasting his time on questions he could never answer. If he could find her, then he could ask her to explain everything to him. After he held her tight in his arms.

"You are worrying about your sister."

Sophia's soft voice brought him back to the moment, and he met her sympathetic gaze. "I am. I feel as if she is just out of reach, if only I can . . ."

She leaned in and kissed his jaw, nuzzling against the prickly beard he had growing. "Gordon will discover what happened. He is determined to give you the answer."

He ran his hand over her hair. "I wish he didn't think he owed me anything. I only did what anyone else would do when we were at school."

"Nicholas," she said gently, "that wasn't what anyone else would do. You were kind to him, and you stood up to bullies. He would not have turned out to be the man he is if you had not looked after him. Life can be hard and cruel. I know from experience how some people enjoy dragging one down, and without you that would have happened to him."

He stroked a finger over her soft cheek. "Your life with Oldney must have been miserable."

"Sometimes it was, but I thought it was what I wanted, convinced myself it was what I wanted. To be the queen of the *ton*, to attend every ball and soiree, and be envied by the rest. I have only recently learned that is not what I want. Or perhaps I have finally grown up from the girl who married Oldney."

"I wish . . ." He began, but he didn't want to say the words yet. He wasn't ready, and he reminded himself that he must not act rashly. So he smiled instead and brushed his lips against hers. "I should go. We will meet again, at Lucifer's."

She nodded seriously. "Yes." It sounded like a vow. "Don't be late! I have a feeling . . ."

He waited for her to finish the sentence, but she had climbed out of bed and turned away, busily filling the basin with water to wash in. Did she have an intuition that something would happen tonight? He had had similar feelings himself, so he knew not to disregard them.

"I won't be late," he said quietly. "You can rely on me, Sophia."

She did not answer him. Perhaps she did not hear him, or perhaps she felt too vulnerable to face him.

Hurriedly, Nicholas dressed and slipped out of the door of the bedchamber. There was no one in the passage, and he made his way to the stairs. As he descended he could hear someone approaching along the corridor from the back of the house, and he leaped the last two stairs and was out the door before they appeared. No matter how blasé Sophia was about him staying overnight, he didn't want to cause her any more problems.

Outside, the sun was well up in the sky and it was a glorious day. He took a moment to breathe in deeply of the fresh air. He felt . . . different. Part of him was happy to just be alive—an unusual state of affairs for him—while the other part was twisted with anxiety about Fern and Gordon. And Sophia. He reminded himself that he was good at this, and all he really needed to do was make certain he was there when she needed him.

In the meantime, why not allow himself a moment of happiness? He was in love, and Nicholas had never been in love before. It was wondrous and most surprising.

But already other thoughts were crowding in, reminding him that in his thirty-two years he had rarely been truly happy. The burdens of other people had always rested heavily upon his shoulders. It might explain the gray hairs he had begun to find among the dark ones on his head.

Was this love something he could trust, even in himself? He used to dislike Sophia so intensely, and yet he had always been drawn to her. Now he was so enchanted with her, he rather thought he would do whatever she asked of him.

Loving her was wondrous, yes, but it also made him vulnerable, and Nicholas wasn't sure if that was a good thing.

Chapter Sixteen

W HEN SOPHIA ARRIVED the next night at Lucifer's—the hell was tucked away in a narrow street on the edge of St. Giles—the first thing she heard was Chatham's bored drawl.

"There you are, Madam. I beg you to put your skills to use. Robinson is on a winning streak, and the three of us will soon be paupers."

She smiled as if she were amused, but it was becoming more and more difficult to play her part. She wanted nothing more than to stand up and leave and return to Berkeley Square and wait for Nicholas. She had glanced about her on the way inside and hadn't seen him, but she knew how clever he was at hiding himself in plain sight.

For a time, the four of them played, and at one point she rose to fetch them a plate of biscuits to nibble on. She thought Gordon could do with soaking up his few sips of wine, and the table service at Lucifer's left a great deal to be desired. Why hadn't the others gone to Hettie Devenish's as usual? Apart from Hettie warning them about Gordon—at least that was what Sophia assumed she'd done—was there a reason they were now at Lucifer's? It only took her a short while to notice that the play at Lucifer's was more dangerously deep than at other clubs. Gentlemen hunched over their cards, as if they had only one aim in their lives, and that was to win. She recognized some of them, highfliers from the government who should have known better.

Questions plagued her, and when she returned to the table she was still so deep in her own thoughts that she missed part of the conversation.

"Then we are agreed?" Chatham was exchanging glances with the other two men, and they shared smiles.

All except Gordon, who swallowed, his gaze skimming over Sophia as if he didn't want it to linger too obviously. "Are you sure it is a good idea?" he said. "I did not hear the insult you spoke of, and the Earl of Mountfitchet is friends with the Prime Minister. He won't take kindly to me—to me . . ." His voice trailed off, and he covered his mouth as if he might be sick.

"What insult?" Sophia asked, but they weren't listening.

Butcher made a sound of disgust, and Arnold joined him. Chatham was watching Gordon with a disappointed look in his blue eyes. "I thought you were a man, Robinson. Am I wrong?"

"I just—"

"*What* insult?" Sophia demanded, cutting across Gordon's protest. "What are you talking about?"

The marquess looked mildly surprised. "You did not hear it? As you walked past Mountfitchet over there," he nodded toward one of the gentlemen she had recognized at the next table bar one, "he made a slighting reference to you. We all heard it, and young Robinson here is going to avenge your honor."

Sophia stared at Chatham. *Avenge her honor?* It sounded ridiculous, and not something the marquess was in the habit of doing. She had been insulted before, and usually they just laughed it off. Although now she thought about it, there had been an incident once when someone said something unpleasant in front of Oldney, and the next time she saw the gentleman, he'd had a black eye.

Perhaps they *were* prepared to stand up for her and she was being unnecessarily skeptical. And yet there was something in the air around them that made her suspicious.

She looked at Gordon and noticed how pale he was, before she turned back to the marquess. "Do you mean a duel?" Her voice was far too loud, and she was quickly shushed by the others.

"No, not a *duel*," Chatham hissed. "Duels are illegal, as you well know, Duchess. We will meet with him and demand an apology, and if he refuses then we will teach him a lesson. Robinson is hot for it, are you not, boy?"

Gordon looked sick, and certainly not ready to take on a man of twice his age and experience. And as he had said, an important man high in the government. But he could not refuse outright. This may be a test of his loyalty to the group.

Or what if this was the plan Chatham had spoken of? The way in which they were going to ruin Gordon? Her stomach dropped in a dizzying fashion. Yes, it made sense. Gordon would "teach" the earl a lesson, and there would be a tremendous scandal. A scuffle between Gordon and Mountfitchet might be forgiven, but what if Mountfitchet was injured? Gordon would go to prison, unless he asked Nicholas with his powerful friends to step in and intervene with the earl and the government. Even if he rescued Gordon, he would never be looked upon the same again. Involving himself with the Duke of Oldney's widow and her compatriots? How could Nicholas maintain his good standing?

No wonder Gordon looked so frightened. If he refused, then his time with the set was over and so was any chance he had of discovering what had happened to Fern.

No, he had to go through with it, and just pray that Nicholas was watching on, and would swoop in like an avenging angel and save them before too much damage was done.

"Well?" Sir Tomas said, his face close to Gordon's. "There is a sniff of the coward about you, Robinson."

"Downright chicken-hearted," Butcher added, sneering.

Gordon swallowed and straightened his back, his jaw jutting out in a pugnacious manner. "I will do it. I can't allow the duchess to be insulted, no matter who the man is. The blighter," he added, and his voice gave an unfortunate squeak.

"Good fellow!" The marquess clapped him so heartily on the back he almost fell into his drink. "I knew you would step up. Look at him, he's ready for anything!"

Sophia took in their smirking faces. "Really?" she said, because she could not help it. "There is no need for this. I am not bothered by what men say, especially those who mean nothing to me. My skin is thicker than that."

Gordon's eyes met hers, and there was a spark of hope in them. But the others weren't having it and refused to be turned from their objective.

"Men like that think they are above the rest of us, and can do and say as they wish," Sir Tomas hissed furiously. "It cannot be allowed." His choice of words struck Sophia as strange and hypocritical, as he had accused Nicholas, the commoner, of not showing them enough respect.

"Hear, hear," Lord Butcher thumped his fist on the table, making the cards and the goblets jump. "Robinson will make him change his tune."

Sophia knew then that this was going to happen and there was nothing she could do to stop it.

Gordon got to his feet and made his way to Mountfitchet's table. There was evidently some deep play going on there and no one seemed to notice him standing there. He cleared his throat and eventually the earl looked up. He frowned, scanning Gordon's face with disinterest.

"What do you want?" he asked, choosing another card from the deck.

"You insulted the Dowager Duchess of Oldney," Gordon said. He glanced back at Sophia and then took a breath and put his hand on Mountfitchet's shoulder. "I am here to avenge her honor."

"You're what?" One of the earl's companions goggled at him. "Are you foxed, boy? Do you know who you're speaking to?"

"The man who insulted a lady," Gordon responded, and his voice had gained strength. He was getting into his role and Sophia wanted to shake him.

She watched in dismay as the earl rose to his feet, throwing aside his cards. "I will pretend I did not hear you, and for your sake you should be grateful," he said slowly. He was tall and thin, with a beak of a nose, and he must be twice Gordon's age. But there was nothing feeble about him, and from the looks of anticipation on the faces of his friends, he was well able to take care of himself.

"I can't do that," Gordon replied bravely. Beads of sweat were popping up on his brow.

Mountfitchet stared at him a moment more and then shrugged. "Let's deal with this now then. I don't remember saying anything derogatory about the lady, but if you say I did . . ." He smiled, and Sophia realized then that the earl was actually looking forward to this. "There's a courtyard near here where we can settle our argument."

Mountfitchet stalked out of the room, which was deadly quiet now, everyone watching on. No chance of pretending this wasn't happening. His friends rose to follow him, and Chatham and the others rose, too, with Sophia following them. Her legs felt as if they could barely hold her up, and when she reached Gordon, he clung to her arm as if he were close to fainting. She managed to be alone with him briefly, while his coat and her cloak were fetched.

"You do not have to do this," she said, leaning in close. "We can say no and walk away. This isn't helping us find Fern."

His eyes were wide, and he looked so young. It broke her heart. "But how will we ever find her if I *don't* do this?" he said. Then, catching Chatham's gaze upon them, he raised his voice. "I refuse to let that man insult you, Your Grace. He needs to be taught a lesson."

Sophia shrugged indifferently. "I'm sure it wasn't meant," she said.

"He called you a harlot," Arnold replied, and there was glee in his eyes. "*Our* harlot. He wondered aloud if you took us on one at a time or all together."

Sophia felt sick. "Nasty," she said, her voice not as confident as before. "I'm sorry I did not to hear him. I would have dealt with him myself."

Sir Tomas patted her on the shoulder with false sympathy. "Well now you don't have to," he said. "If Oldney were here, he would do the same."

"In fact," Lord Butcher looked about at them, "we will do this in Oldney's name. He was our friend, and you were his wife."

Sophia tried to look grateful. She tied her cloak, purposely dropping her money purse, and using the moment to glance about her. Some of the other patrons had followed them out, eager to watch the spectacle. But where was Nicholas?

He must be here somewhere. He said he would be. Why couldn't she see him? It felt as if everything had happened too quickly and they weren't ready. Gordon was scared to death and her hands were shaking. She hoped Nicholas was prepared to step in when the time came, or they would be in trouble.

When she finished with her cloak and looked up, Chatham was watching her with a satisfied smirk on his face. He immediately changed his expression to a concerned one, but it made no difference to how she felt about him. He knew exactly what he was doing.

"I still think an apology will suffice," she said. "I will ask him for one."

Chatham's hand grasped her wrist so tightly that it hurt. She tried to pull away, but he would not release her. "I don't think that is wise, Duchess," he said quietly, but there was a warning in his pale eyes. "It will not send the message we desire. Mount-fitchet must learn his lesson. Would you deny Robinson here the opportunity to behave in a heroic manner?"

"Of course not," she said impatiently, giving her hand another tug. This time Chatham released it. "But nor do I want blood shed over a—a trifle."

"Your honor is no trifle, Madam," Sir Tomas said gravely, as if he knew what honor was. "We are prepared to uphold it no matter the cost."

Dear God, this was madness, but there seemed nothing she could do to stop it. Even Gordon was determined to go through with it. She just had to hope that Nicholas was nearby and could stop them.

"Very well," she snapped. "If you must."

They exchanged more glances, while Gordon fiddled with his cuffs. This was it then, the plot that would bring Nicholas down. It felt as if it was rushing toward her like a runaway carriage, and she wasn't sure she would have time to step aside before it struck her.

Chapter Seventeen

NICHOLAS WAS LATE arriving at Lucifer's. An important government official, or so the man believed himself to be, had arrived at his rooms just as he was getting ready to head out. He was forced to linger and make polite conversation. In the way of most of the "important" government officials he was acquainted with, it seemed impossible for him to get to the point.

Nicholas longed to tell him to get out, but some of his most lucrative cases came from this fellow, and so he waited. And waited. Until eventually he was able to escape and rushed off to Lucifer's.

Only to find them gone.

As luck would have it, however, they hadn't left quietly and unobtrusively. The people Nicholas spoke to knew what had happened and where they had gone, along with quite a few curious observers.

Nicholas wasn't that far behind them, and he tried not to panic. He set off at a brisk pace, past a number of lanes and rickety buildings. This part of London was home to rookeries and slums, and although he couldn't see anyone watching him, he was certain they were there. At least Sophia had been with a group and would be safe, for now. And what of Gordon? Would Mountfitchet kill him if he could? The earl had a reputation for teaching his detractors a lesson, as he called it, and he didn't hold back.

He wondered, too, if this was the plan Chatham and the others had had all along. And now he was late. They were relying upon him, and he had let them down. He wouldn't blame Sophia if she was so angry about his tardiness that she never wanted to see him again.

"Damn it!" he shouted, startling some children sitting on a doorstep. Where was this place?

"Sir, sir!" one of them called. "Can you spare a penny?"

He could barely spare the time, not really, but with a sigh he walked over to them and searched in his pocket. "You haven't seen some gentlemen and a lady pass by?" he asked, as he held the coin out, not expecting to hear good news.

"Yes, sir, we did," the child said with a grin. His face was dirty, but his smile was brilliant. "Does that mean we get two pennies?"

Nicholas searched desperately in his pocket. "A shilling . . . two shillings," he declared recklessly.

The boy pointed back the way he had come. "They went into the cul-de-sac," he said. "We aren't allowed to go down there— everyone knows it ain't safe. Sometimes there's fisty cuffs down there, or gents with swords."

Nicholas looked at the entrance to the narrow alley and felt his heart sink. But he gave out the reward and thanked the children before he began to jog.

He heard voices, the murmur of a small crowd, and then Chatham calling out.

"Wait until I give the signal!"

"Why should I listen to you?" It was Mountfitchet, a sneer in his voice. "First you lie about what I said, and then you bring this beardless boy to fight me."

Nicholas's eyes adjusted to the gloom, and he could see a circle of people, with Gordon and Mountfitchet in the middle. Chatham was leaning on his cane, and close beside him was

Sophia, her gaze fixed on the two men.

"This is insanity," one of the earl's group said loudly. "Are you really going to do this, Mountfitchet?"

"I didn't start it," the earl retorted.

"We all heard you insult the duchess," Chatham said. "You cannot lie your way out of it. You need to be punished, sir. Robinson, hand him his weapon."

The earl pointed at Sophia. "I did nothing of the sort, but even if I did insult her it would be justifiable. Anyone with the name Oldney is a disgrace. Now this is your last chance. Let me pass and we will say no more about it."

"Too late for that!" Was that Arnold? "Come, Robinson, on guard!"

There was a laugh in his voice, as if it was all a game to him, and Nicholas went cold. Gordon was no fencer, at least he hadn't been when Nicholas had known him best. Now he could hear Sophia's voice, but not what she was saying. She seemed to be arguing with them. There was the sound of steel clashing—good God they were really going to fight!—and then a cry of pain.

In a flash, Nicholas was running, pushing his way through the crowd, which was larger than he had thought.

There was a flaring torch held by a lamplighter who had been pulled into the situation, and it shone on the faces, gleaming in their eyes and giving everything a nightmare quality. Sophia lifted her head, almost as if she had sensed him arrive, her face a white oval within the hood of her dark cloak. Before he could call out, there was another clash of steel.

"Stop!" he shouted, but it was too late.

Even as everyone froze and turned to stare, one of the men in the center slumped to the ground.

"What do you want, Blake?" Chatham said. "Have you come to champion your apprentice?" The words were chosen for Mountfitchet's ears, chosen to cause the most trouble.

"You know this young fellow?" Mountfitchet demanded, striding closer. His eyes blazed in the firelight. "If I find you have had anything to do with this, I will speak directly to the Prime Minister. You will never work for us again."

It was exactly what Chatham and his crew were hoping for, but Nicholas did not have time to argue. He could see now that it was indeed Gordon who had been hurt. He was sitting on the wet cobbles with his head bent and holding his arm. Sophia was kneeling beside him.

"Nicholas," she said. "Thank God."

There was a hiss from Chatham at her words, but it took him only an instant to use them to his advantage. "Young Robinson here is Blake's protégé, and my dear Dowager Duchess of Oldney is his mistress. Ask him!"

Nicholas shot them a look of pure disgust before he turned to Mountfitchet and his friends. "I came here tonight to put a stop to this madness, but I was too late. Chatham hates me more than most, and he concocted a plan to see me ruined by using my foolish young friend here. I don't think it was particularly well thought out, but I am guessing Gordon would soon have found himself in a seriously awkward situation over this evening's events and asked for my help, and then it would have been assumed I would help him and have my reputation destroyed."

Chatham made a huffing sound. "What nonsense!"

"Who are you to tell us what to do?" Butcher sneered. "A commoner!"

"A commoner and a reverend's son!" Arnold added sourly.

"Blake?" the earl asked imperiously, resting on the point of his sword. "Is this true? It is so ridiculous that I find it hard to believe sensible men would do such a thing."

Gordon raised his head, still clutching his arm. There was the shine of blood on his fingers. "I went to the same school as Nicholas Blake. Sir Tomas has just said he was the reverend's son, and he's right. He knows because his brother Joseph went to that school, too."

Nicholas moved closer and Arnold seemed to struggle to stand his ground. His heart was beating with a hard, fast rhythm, but he kept himself under control. "What happened to Fern? Tell me now and perhaps you won't have to flee the country."

"Who on earth is 'Fern'?" Arnold spat, but there was a note in his voice that gave him away.

"My sister," Nicholas said, his voice quietly ominous.

"Your sister?" Mountfitchet looked uneasy. He glanced back to his fellows and then to Sir Tomas. "I don't like the sound of this. It has a whiff of serious scandal. Why do you think Arnold knows what happened to your sister, Blake?"

"Because he was the last to see her. What sort of 'gentleman' makes off with an innocent seventeen-year-old girl? What did you do to her? I swear I will see you and your friends ruined if you don't tell me."

Mountfitchet's voice was suddenly very grave. "I would tell him if I were you."

Arnold made another scoffing sound, as if he was about to deny everything, but Chatham caught his arm and moved so that their faces were very close. "Tell him," he said angrily. "What does it matter now? No one cares about the silly chit. Tell him."

Arnold nodded and drew away, his fists clenched and his voice tight with anger. "Very well, but there is little to tell. She came with me willingly, and she was my mistress for a year. She was happy with the arrangement, there was no force involved. I was fond of her until she began to whine about marriage. I got rid of her after that."

Nicholas moved toward him purposefully.

"No!" Sophia cried out, and rising swiftly to her feet, she pressed her hands to his chest. "He knows." To Arnold she said, "What happened to her?"

Arnold stared at Nicholas a moment as if he was going to tell them, but then he met Chatham's gaze again and gave a nonchalant shrug. "Who knows? I presume she found someone else." His gaze slid to Sophia, and he smirked. "Girls like that are ten a penny. They don't mind who beds them, as long as they have a roof over their heads."

"You're lying," Sophia said. "I know what the truth looks like on your face, and this isn't it. Where is she? There's more to this story. Something is missing and . . ."

"If you have harmed her," Nicholas interrupted with a growl, "I will hunt you down. There won't be anywhere you can hide."

"I'm not lying," he blustered. "She left. That is all I know."

"It seems you are at a stalemate," Mountfitchet said thoughtfully. "I could look into the matter, but the girl has been gone how long?"

"Nine years," Sir Tomas said. "She could be anywhere."

Mountfitchet sighed. "There is not much to be done then, Blake." He looked about him. "I will take your word that none of this is your doing, but my patience is at an end with you all. My advice to you, Chatham, is to rusticate in the country. The Prime Minister may not be as eager to forget as I am. Blake is his pet, and he won't take kindly to your treatment of him."

Chatham jerked his cuffs into place. "Very well," he said. "I will take your advice. My country house is calling to me." He turned to Sophia, and she could see his eyes glittering with fury, but he hid it well. "You disappoint me, Duchess. I thought you had better taste. We wasted our time trying to avenge your honor—you did not deserve Oldney."

Sophia said nothing, staring back at him. She watched as the three men walked away. The rest followed, eager to get back to their gaming now that the show was over. A cat slunk out of the shadows, hissed, and ran on. She met Nicholas's eyes and there was an urgency about her, as if something important had just occurred to her, but there was no time now for a tête-à-tête.

Gordon was trying to get to his feet, and Nicholas reached down to hoist him up. "We must get you a doctor," Sophia said.

"I can't believe I let him under my guard," Gordon muttered.

"He's a practiced swordsman, and you are not," Nicholas said, with a touch of humor. His smile died. "I wasn't here to stop it, and I'm sorry for that."

"You are not my nursemaid," Gordon retorted savagely. "I

chose to go with them."

"So did I," Sophia said, looking at Nicholas as if daring him to reprimand her. "At least this game is over. Do you think they will be punished?"

"Probably not. Unless being in the country for the foreseeable future will be punishment enough for men like them. Now that Mountfitchet knows the story he might help if I want to take it further, but I can only do that if I find Fern."

Gordon groaned, clutching his arm. "I am so sorry I didn't find out where she went after Arnold. I've mucked it up."

"You did more than I could," Nicholas retorted. "At least we know now what happened to her after she left the school. And I can't believe Arnold when he says he doesn't know where she went. Those three are close. One of them might have taken her as his mistress. I won't stop looking."

Sophia gave him a sharp glance. She was quiet as they made their way out of the cul-de-sac and back to Lucifer's. She was quiet in the coach, too, and Nicholas found himself turning to her a number of times, wondering if she regretted having anything to do with him. Maybe they were over. His spirits sank even further.

"Gordon!" Sophia was propping Gordon up, with him close to swooning. Nicholas took off his cravat and wrapped it around the wound in the boy's upper arm, to stem the bleeding, but Gordon had already lost a lot of blood.

His thoughts kept returning to his sister. He tried not to think about her life with Arnold, apart from hoping it wasn't too awful. She must have realized shortly after he installed her in that *pied à terre* that he wasn't the love of her life.

What had happened to her afterward? He felt sick at the thought. Had he discovered the truth about her leaving only to face the fact that he was less likely than ever to find her now?

"I will send for the doctor as soon as we arrive," Sophia's voice brought him back to himself. She was watching him from the other side of the coach.

"Thank you," Nicholas said. "And I'm sorry—"

"Oh for God's sake, there's nothing to be sorry about!" Sophia said crossly. "You always do your best, we know that. And you came at the right time, just like some hero in a novel."

He gave an involuntary crack of laughter.

She stared at him, and he could see there was something very wrong. She opened her mouth and then bit her lip, her eyes full of questions.

"What is it?" he said sharply.

"I . . ." She shook her head. "Something has occurred to me. I do not know if I am completely wrong, but I . . ."

"Sophia?" He leaned forward to take her hands, or he would have if Gordon weren't leaning heavily against him. "What is it?"

But at that moment they reached the house.

Chapter Eighteen

SOPHIA WONDERED IF she was going insane. The idea that had gradually unfurled inside her head as she'd stood listening to Arnold talk, seemed preposterous. And yet was it? The way in which Chatham had stared at Arnold when they were asked about the whereabouts of Fern, as if warning him to stay silent spoke volumes. She knew the bare fact that Fern had been Arnold's mistress for a year—that much was established. But then they said she disappeared, only Sophia didn't think that was true. She knew how close Arnold and his friends were, how their lives were so intertwined. She knew of their loyalty to Oldney, even after death.

Was it possible they had shared Arnold's mistress once he'd tired of her?

Had they shared Fern?

She was growing more and more sure of it, but she needed to be careful. She must not be hasty in sharing her conclusion. How disappointed would Nicholas be if she was wrong? And yet despite her need for caution she was certain that she was right.

As Sophia crossed the threshold of her home and removed her gloves. Webster was there to take her outdoor clothing. His eyes widened at the sight of Gordon and his bloodied shirt, and Sophia had barely opened her mouth to order that the doctor be fetched before the butler was shouting for a servant. Poor Webster. She wouldn't be at all surprised if he handed in his notice in the morning.

Nicholas helped Gordon into the Yellow Room, and Sophia tried not to think about her pretty chintz-covered sofa as he slumped down upon it. As she watched the two men, she was considering whether or not to speak aloud what she had been thinking. It was just a shame that Chatham and the others would be on their way to the country by now and could not be questioned further.

"Your Grace? Did you need me? Mr. Webster said you have a person who is injured."

Sophia looked up and saw Marianne, standing in the doorway. She had a robe over her nightdress and her hair was in a braid over her shoulder, and she looked as if she had only just been woken. She stared at the scene before her in consternation, and her gaze went from Sophia to Gordon, and then to Nicholas who was kneeling at his side.

Her dark eyes widened, her face turning so pale that Sophia was sure she was about to faint.

Sophia moved toward her, but she knew then she had been right.

Nicholas staggered to his feet. "Fern?" he cried, his voice hoarse with an overwhelming emotion. "My God, is it you?"

"Nicholas?" Marianne ignored Sophia's outstretched hand and tottered a few steps, resting her weight against the back of an armchair. "Oh." Tears sprang to her eyes and overflowed, pouring down her cheeks. She covered her face with her hands and turned her back. "What must you think of me?" she cried in a broken, muffled voice.

But whatever Nicholas thought, it wasn't what his sister expected. He had reached her in two strides and taken her in his arms, pulling her roughly against him. His head bowed over hers, and Sophia could see that his eyes were shut. "I've found you," he murmured. "At last, at last, I've found you."

Sophia wiped tears from her own cheeks, took a deep breath, and went to pour Gordon some brandy. He was staring at the brother and sister in wonder, but he took the glass and sipped the restorative. He gave Sophia a shaky grin. "You've worked a miracle, Duchess," he said. "How on earth did you manage it?"

Sophia shook her head. "I didn't do anything. I wish I could take credit, but this has been a lucky accident. I did think, earlier tonight, that after Fern left Arnold she was likely with one of the other men. Then I remembered Marianne and Oldney."

By now, Fern had recovered herself a little, and Nicholas, too. He led her over to the sofa and sat her down beside Gordon. She blinked at him in wonder.

"What are *you* doing here?" she asked him. Then back to Nicholas, "And you? I don't understand." And finally, to Sophia, "Did *you* know who I was all along?"

Sophia was quick to deny it. "No, I didn't know. I promise you I didn't." She met Nicholas's dark eyes, so like his sister's now she noticed, and saw the warmth in them.

"Duchess," he whispered.

It wasn't just warmth in his eyes, but love. An abundance of love.

Fern shook her head in bewilderment. "Please, Nicholas, tell me how you are here! Are you and the duchess friends? Why haven't I seen you here before?"

Sophia bit back a smile as she wondered how he would explain the matter, but he was clever enough to do so without bringing their relationship into it. Gordon jumped into the conversation, too, sharing his part in the story, and finally Sophia took over.

"Do you remember that I told you Marianne . . . I mean Fern, was living in Curzon Street?" she said.

Nicholas went very quiet as he realized what she meant, and his face was grave. "You were with Oldney," he spoke at last.

Fern drew herself up tall, as if she refused to be ashamed, and Sophia was impressed by her strength of character. "After I left

Tomas, Oldney took me in. I was with him until he died. We have a son, Hugo." She paused, as if struggling to find the words. "I am sorry, Nicholas. I didn't know you were looking for me. I was never told, although Oldney must have known."

Of course he knew, Sophia thought angrily. He had known and probably enjoyed every moment of it. What revenge upon the man he despised, having his sister as his mistress! She wondered if her husband had considered using Fern if the chance had ever come up, a pawn in his vicious game. And what would Nicholas have done to save her? Sophia suspected there was very little he *wouldn't* have done.

Fern was still speaking in a small, brave voice. "I knew I was in a desperate place when Oldney died, but I couldn't come home. How could I, after what I had done? My reputation was ruined, I was disgraced. The school would have sacked father, and the stain would have followed you both wherever you went. I was sure you must both hate me. I hated myself for a time. But there is Hugo. I have him, and I would never wish him away."

"Of course not," Sophia said, remembering Hugo's sweet smile. "He is yours far more than Oldney's."

"You could have come to me." Nicholas sounded disappointed. "I have been searching for you for years. Father believed that one day we would find you, and even when I almost gave up, I knew I had to continue for his sake. How could you believe we would forget you?"

Fern listened with wide eyes, as if struggling to make sense of it. No doubt she had been told many lies during the last ten years, and it would take time to sort them from the truth.

Sophia took her hand in hers. "You changed your name," she said. "Why did you do that? Did Oldney do it because he thought you would be found?"

"I don't know. I didn't think so. Oldney said he didn't like 'Fern,' so I became Marianne. I was happy to comply, if it kept the peace. It is so long now since anyone has called me Fern. I'd almost forgotten." She bowed her head and began to quietly weep. Sophia wrapped an arm about her, and Nicholas leaned in to dab ineffectually at her face with his handkerchief.

"No one is blaming you for anything," Nicholas said sternly. "I'm sorry we are asking you so many questions, and there will be more, but not now. Now, I am just happy to have you here with me. And I want to meet my nephew as soon as possible."

Fern gave him a grateful smile. "He's very like you. For so long I have wanted you to see him. Once Oldney was gone, I told him about you and father. I didn't before because I knew it would make Oldney angry."

No one answered her. The thought of the life she had lived for the past ten years was too painful for them all. Nicholas might be upset that Fern had not returned to her home, but he was being understanding.

And his long search was over.

Selfishly, Sophia wondered what that meant for her. Would Nicholas leave London for Fern's sake and set up house for them all somewhere far away? If he did, if they all left, Sophia's big house would be empty again, and she wasn't sure she would be able to bear it.

"Your Grace," Webster announced primly from the doorway. "The doctor is here."

Chapter Nineteen

MARIANNE AND NICHOLAS were seated together very close, their voices too low for Sophia to hear, but she smiled whenever she glanced at them. She was exhausted—it had been a fraught few hours—but she was also elated.

Nicholas had found his sister, and Gordon was free from the company of those vile men. And though Oldney had been the vilest of them all, it turned out that Marianne—Fern, she reminded herself—had been reasonably well treated. He had not grown bored with her, as Arnold had, and passed her on to someone else. Someone like Chatham.

Sophia shuddered at the thought of Chatham getting his hands on the sweet girl. And Fern was right, she had Hugo, and Sophia was determined that Oldney's son be given his due. A good school, although perhaps not the sort of school Gordon and Nicholas had been to, and his rightful place in the world.

"Your Grace?"

Sophia blinked. Damn it, had she fallen asleep? "Yes, Marianne . . . I mean, Fern?"

The other woman smiled. Despite her pale face and shadowed eyes, she looked content. "It is very late and if I am to run your house well, I should retire."

"Yes. Of course. We can talk in the morning. You may not

want to stay now that your brother . . ." She looked over at Nicholas.

"I *do* want to stay," Fern said firmly. "You have been so kind to me, and I like it here. Hugo likes it here. If you will have us, then we will stay."

"I will certainly have you both."

Goodnights were spoken. Gordon was already tucked up in one of the guest beds, the doctor having dressed his wound and pronounced it not too serious.

"I'm so glad you found your sister," Sophia began, as soon as the door was closed. "And I'm sorry I didn't realize sooner who she was. It wasn't until Chatham and Mountfitchet were posturing that I had an inkling that perhaps Fern had left Arnold and gone to one of the others. They were always so enmeshed in each other's lives. I wanted to tell you right away, but what if I had been wrong? I'm sorry . . ."

Nicholas gaze softened. "No need, Duchess. I keep thinking that if you had not been so kind as to take her in, I don't know what would have happened to her next." He took a shaky breath, and she could see that the emotional reunion with Fern had taken its toll on him, too. "Truly, Sophia, you are a woman in a million! The sweetest, dearest, kindest—"

This time it was Sophia who laughed. "I think you must be lightheaded, Nicholas. I am none of those things. But I am trying. I want to be kind, to make up for the times I was not so kind. I give my sister, Ellis, credit for the change in me. She made me realize that people only see what you show them. You may mean well but how can they know if you do not invite them into your heart?"

He came and sat beside her, taking her hands in his. "A bit like you and me," he said gently. "Our dislike of each other became a habit."

She wondered what he was going to say. He had a look on his face that made her think he was working up to something. She only hoped he wasn't going to bid her farewell and ride off into the distance.

"Sophia, I have wanted to tell you this for days now, but I didn't know if you would welcome the words." He took a breath. "I love you. And no, I have not lost my mind. I love you, and if you don't want to hear that, then too bad."

He looked so stubborn, almost as if he were expecting the worst. Nicholas had not had an entirely happy life thus far, at least not the sort of life he deserved. But Sophia was determined that only good things would come his way from now on. She would make sure of it, starting now.

She leaned forward and rested her forehead against his. "I love you, too. Are we not a pair? Who would have thought? Who will believe it when they hear? Nicholas Blake and the Dowager Duchess of Oldney in love and delighted about it."

"You love me?" he breathed. And then, with a frown, "Who cares what anyone else thinks? Unless . . . do you? Will the *ton* disapprove?"

"Probably. And I do not care. I am deliriously happy to have you, and everyone else can go to hell."

He kissed her, gently, as if she had said something profound. When he slipped his arm about her, she rested her head on his shoulder.

"What shall we do next?" she asked him dreamily. "Please don't ask me for another favor, especially if it means I have to enter a gambling hell."

He laughed. "I promise you I won't. I have been thinking for some time that I would be happy to retire. It is a wearing and lonely life. And my father is getting old, and I want to live closer to him. But it would mean moving to Hampshire." He pulled a face. "I suspect that is not what you want at all, is it?"

Sophia thought a moment. "I would not mind," she answered honestly, because it was true. "Oldney had a number of houses which are now sitting empty and costing me a great deal—I cannot tell you how badly he managed his estates! I was considering selling some of them, and if I did that we could buy something closer to your father."

"I have savings you know," he said, sounding stern. "I am well paid for my work, so I do not expect to sponge off you, Duchess."

As if she would ever believe him capable of such a thing. She took his hand in hers and squeezed it. "We will share," she said. "What is mine is yours and what is yours is mine. Although . . ."

He groaned. "Sophia, I don't expect—"

"I assure you, I am perfectly happy with such an arrangement," she said, and gazed into his eyes so that he could see she was in earnest. "But I was thinking of Marianne and Hugo. She seems happy to remain here for now, and I will let her settle before I broach the subject, but Nicholas, I want Hugo to take his rightful place in the world. He is Oldney's son. He should have the estate in Surrey—it has been in the Oldney family for generations. I will keep this place, too, so that when we come to London we will all have somewhere to stay. Do you think that is a good idea?"

He was gazing at her as if she was so wonderful he could not find the words. It made her uncomfortable because Sophia knew all too well her many faults. He would find them out once the gloss had begun to wear off, but it was nice that at least for the moment he believed her to be a saint.

"Yes, I think it a very good idea," he said. "I love you so much. I sometimes wonder if I always did, even while I was loathing you."

She laughed aloud now. "Come, Nicholas, that is ridiculous. I certainly didn't love you until you showed yourself to me truly. I thought you an arrogant snake, and I said so many times. Just ask Ellis."

He smoothed her hair back, gazing into her face. "This is the beginning for us, isn't it? A new life?"

"Yes. A new life," she whispered.

And then he was kissing her again, warm and loving, and when the tingle of desire began to burn in them both, Sophia led him upstairs to her bedchamber.

Epilogue

Two years later

THEY HAD ARRIVED in Berkeley Square from the country this morning, and Sophia wanted nothing more than to lie on her bed and sleep until her stomach settled. Fern and Hugo would be here soon, as well as Ellis and Owen, and Catherine and Albury, with their families. And as much as she was looking forward to seeing them all, right now she wanted nothing more than peace and quiet.

"The screaming and crying, the pounding of feet up and down the stairs!" she had said to Nicholas, which made him laugh.

"Are you not fond of your nieces and nephews?" he had asked with a grin.

"In moderation."

"Then it is just as well we do not have any of our own," he had said.

There had been an uncomfortable pause. She had felt the tension in his arm where it was tucked around her shoulders, and she had not dared to meet his eyes.

Not a good start, she told herself now, trying to get comfortable on her bed.

Nicholas had headed off to Westminster soon after, and she wasn't sure what he was up to. Some secret government business. Far from retiring, he was still engaged in his work. He wasn't quite as diligent as before, but he had told her that he had to do something now his time was not taken up searching for his missing sister.

"Although it was you who found Fern," he always said, with a smile. He still smiled at her as if she was his everything.

Sophia closed her eyes with a groan and lay perfectly still on the bed. She felt queasy from the coach journey, at least that was what she had told Nicholas. Sophia had had her suspicions for some months now but hadn't wanted to say anything in case she was wrong. Well, she wasn't wrong.

She was with child. Nicholas's child. The idea filled her with a sense of trepidation and wonder. Wonder because Sophia had wanted a child ever since she had watched Ellis with her newborn daughter. But she had given up on having a child of her own. All those years with Oldney and then two more years with Nicholas, and nothing. And it wasn't as if she and Nicholas hadn't spent many rigorous and enjoyable hours doing their best to reproduce. Recently she had begun to accept the fact that their lives would be lived without a baby of their own. And what did it matter really? They had Hugo, and her nieces and nephews.

She and Nicholas were very happy together. Even if she suspected he would like a little Blake to carry on his name, he had promised her he was perfectly content.

And trepidation? Well that was because of his comment earlier, about it being just as well they did not have a child of their own. Was she wrong about him wanting a child? Would he be glad or just pretend to be glad? What would he say?

Either way, Sophia could not wait any longer. The baby was due in five months. She would have to break the news to him when he returned from Westminster and before the others arrived. Her sisters would know at once she was reproducing, and she could not let Nicholas learn the news secondhand. By then she hoped she would be feeling less queasy. With a smile, she drifted off to sleep.

NICHOLAS BOUNDED UP the stairs. They had kept him too long at Westminster, but he had finally escaped. He knew he should be flattered that the Prime Minister believed him to be indispensable, but sometimes he wished there was someone else they could call on in an emergency. Thank goodness Gordon was at his side, a sort of apprentice, with the assumption that one day he would take Nicholas's place entirely.

Quietly he opened the bedchamber door.

Sophia was lying curled up on the bed, her eyes closed, her hair loosened, the bedcovers tucked around her. This bed had seen a lot of happy moments between them, and he often thought of the early days, when they had fallen in love. He wasn't sure what he had expected to happen, but he supposed children had come into his thoughts. But he refused to be sad about not having any, because Sophia was more than enough for him.

Nicholas was sorry he had upset her earlier. She did not speak to him about her own disappointment on that score, but he suspected that was how she felt, and with her family descending on them, it would hurt even more.

Her steady breathing suggested she was asleep. Nicholas shouldn't wake her—she had been deep in her own thoughts lately and restless at night. Again, he suspected it was this family reunion that was weighing on her mind. Perhaps he could interest her in another charity by way of distraction? Sophia and Fern were always busy with ways in which to help the less fortunate. He was very grateful that his sister and his wife were so close.

He had long ago put aside the heartbreak of his sister's disappearance and forgiven her for not coming to him for help. He understood why she hadn't, and he was just glad she had returned to him. Chatham and his friends had returned to London briefly only to be banished again by Mountfitchet and the Prime Minister once Fern's story was told to them. It was not widely known, and Nicholas was glad of that—he did not want his sister gossiped about by the *ton*.

As if she sensed his presence, Sophia's eyes flickered open. As soon as she saw him, her face lit up in a smile.

"Nicholas. At last."

He chuckled as he climbed up beside her, lying on his side and reaching to fold her hands against his chest. "I've only been gone a couple of hours. And I told them I will not be available for the next two days."

She pulled a face. "Two days? You will have to do better than that when . . ." Her voice drifted off. "The house will be awfully noisy when everyone arrives tonight," she said quickly, and he wondered at the change in subject.

"I don't mind that," he said, watching her curiously. Was she thinking of what he had said earlier? "You know how fond I am of your sisters and their husbands. As for the children, I know they can be noisy and demanding, but we love them. Don't we?"

"Yes," she whispered, and her eyes filled with tears.

Nicholas was worried now. "What is it?" he asked anxiously and leaned in to kiss her brow. "Duchess? Tell me, please. I can't bear to see you unhappy. Whatever it is . . . we can face it together. I truly believe we can face anything if we are together."

She gave a watery chuckle. "I hope so, Nicholas. Because the child we are going to have is part of us both."

He wasn't sure he had heard her right, but she was watching him intently, looking as if she might start weeping in earnest, and he knew he wasn't mistaken. Nicholas was not the sort of man to usually become overemotional. He liked to think he was steady. So it was to the household's amazement when they heard the duchess's husband shouting at the top of his voice.

Sophia was shaking with laughter. "Nicholas! Hush! They will think . . . well, I don't know what they will think."

He held her to him and kissed her once, twice, and then again. "I am over the moon, Sophia. I don't think I have been this happy since our wedding day. Are you . . .?" He leaned back and his dark gaze searched hers.

Her brown eyes were shining with joy. "Oh yes," she said, "so am I. There was a time when I thought . . . when I feared we would never . . ." Her lip trembled.

He wrapped his arms about her and held her close to his heart. "You know as long as we have each other I am happy, but this . . ." He looked at her again, his expression full of wonder.

"I waited, to make sure," she said. "I didn't quite believe it."

"When will he be born?" he asked.

"She. It may be a 'she.'"

"I don't care, my love. When will this amazing child of ours be born?

She laughed at his worried look. "Not immediately, don't worry. In the summer. We can stay in the country. There will be no trips to Westminster, either. Gordon can deal with that."

Nicholas lifted her hand to his lips. "Yes, Duchess," he said with a grin.

They cuddled together in the warmth of the bed, whispering of the future and their happiness.

Soon the others arrived, and there were tears of joy and congratulations. At dinner, Nicholas rose to his feet at the head of the long table and lifted his glass.

"To the Mallory sisters," he said, with an affectionate smile at the faces smiling back at him. "The Disgraceful Duchesses!"

Laughter and then glasses were lifted high in response.

"To the Disgraceful Duchesses!"

About the Author

Sara Bennett is an Australian bestselling author of Historical Romance. She has written many books set in various time periods—Medieval, Regency and Victorian—as well as Paranormal Romance under the name Sara Mackenzie.

She started her career writing under the penname Deborah Miles for Mills & Boon. Her books have been published by Avon / Harper Collins, and are available worldwide. She has also written numerous Australian Women's Fiction books as Kaye Dobbie. Currently she alternates between publishing independently and with traditional publishers.

Sara has been a finalist for the RITA award (Romance Writers of America) and the RUBY (Romance Writers of Australia).

Sara lives in Victoria, Australia, in an old house in a goldrush town, with her husband and two important cats. She would love to spend more time in the garden but there are just too many stories to be written.

9 781965 539330